Praise for The So

"The Song Spinner will delight readers of all ages... them with much material for serious thought." *Kliatt (U.S.)*

"... an enjoyable, well-woven fantasy." *Vancouver Sun*

"This is a fantasy novel, a little unlike anything else you've read." *Toronto Star*

"... the language of The Song Spinner with Dickensian names and dramatic passages filled with dialogue begs to be read aloud." *Edmonton Journal*

"... a charming fantasy novel." *London Free Press*

"Thank you for a story that will be in my mind and heart forever." *Raquel Bennett, grade 5, Unsworth Elementary, Chilliwack, BC*

"Aurora's journey is a very hopeful one. The most powerful theme of The Song Spinner is the importance of allowing ourselves to speak, sing, express our deep selves. Repressing our voices or the voices of others destroys happiness and inner peace. Honest self-expression empowers us." *Helen Siourbas, Teacher, English Department, Champlain Regional College*

"The rich fantasy land created by Le Bel continues the long tradition of storytellers who recognize that it is children who dream of other worlds, better worlds, and that by ignoring, or worse, suppressing these dreams, we belittle ourselves and narrow our world." *Arts Bridge*

Praise for The Song Spinner movie:

"Enchanting fable..." **** *Martin and Porter Video Movie Guide 1998*

"... a delightfully subversive yarn ... this is a rare production: an entertaining movie for youngsters that treats them with respect and is driven by challenging, even provocative, ideas." *Edmonton Journal*

"A gentle, artistic and powerful portrayal of honoring the truth even when it's forbidden or not popular. It's also about the ability of one courageous heart to affect the world." *Amazon.com*

More —>

"Timeless and timely. A story to touch the hearts of both young and old alike." *Amazon.com*

"This is a beautiful movie for any music lover and a great story for the whole family." *Amazon.com*

"THE SONG SPINNER is a modest wonder, a dramatic parable that doesn't indulge in special-effects glitz or childish whimsy. The moody treatment respects the serious subject matter of tyranny and artistic suppression, even if the sense of danger is low." *TV Guide Review*

Awards for The Song Spinner movie:

Emmy nomination for Best Writing in a Children's Special (**Pauline Le Bel**)

Emmy nomination for Best Children's Special

Emmy nomination for Best Performance by an actress (**Patti Lupone**)

Winner of a Cable ACE Award for Best Writing, Los Angeles (**Pauline Le Bel**)

Winner of the Children's Jury Award, Chicago International Children's Film Festival

Winner of the Gordon Parsons Children's Choice Award for Best Feature, Atlantic Film Festival

Winner of the Bronze, Cairo International Film Festival

Winner of the Children's Choice Award, Cine Junior Festival, Paris France

Winner of the Premio Bico, Festival International de Cine Para Ninos y Jovenes, Montevideo, Uruguay

Winner of the Prix Special, Festival International de Cinema Jeune Public de Laon, France

Winner of the Prix du Jury des Enfants, Cine Junior Festival Jeune Public, Val de Marne

Winner of the Prix du Service de la Jeunesse de Hainaut, Belgium

Honorable Mention, Feature Film, Chicago International Film Festival

THE SONG SPINNER

IN THE LAND OF PINDROP, SILENCE IS NOT ONLY GOLDEN — IT'S THE LAW

PAULINE LE BEL

Trafford Publishing

Originally published by Red Deer Press, Alberta, Canada in 1994.

THANKS to Paul Fast for setting the song spinner spinning again; Will Husby for layout and design; Judy Willoughby-Price for the enchanting cover painting; Roger Willoughby-Price for cover design; and Merna Summers, Monica Hughes, Mike Ross, Randy Bradshaw, and Doug Macleod who heard the music from the very beginning.

Author photograph by Grant Olson

Original financial support provided by the Alberta Foundation for the Arts, the Canada Council, the Department of Communications, Red Deer College, and the Banff Centre for the Arts.

CANADIAN CATALOGUING IN PUBLICATION DATA
    Le Bel, Pauline,
    The Song spinner
    [1. Music-Fiction 2. Magic-Fiction 3. Fantasy]
    I. Title.
    ISBN: 978-1-4251-7462-0
    Fourth printing 2008

Note for Librarians: A cataloguing record for this book is available from Library and Archives Canada at www.collectionscanada.ca/amicus/index-e.html

Trafford PUBLISHING® www.trafford.com

10 9 8 7 6 5 4 3 2

For all those who have been silenced
and who found the courage to speak their own music

Pauline Le Bel is an international award-winning writer
and singer who has performed in theatres and concert halls
across Canada, in the U.S. and the U.K. Reviewers called her "a
musical instrument linked to a soul" and "a national treasure."
The Song Spinner was born out of the sounds and silences of
her own life, and is based on her screenplay which received an
Emmy nomination and a Cable ACE Award for Best Writing in a
Children's Special.

Pauline has also written musicals, radio dramas, songs
for films, and has three CDs of her own songs. Her musical
interpretation of the science-based Universe Story has delighted
and inspired international audiences. Pauline lives on Canada's
west coast where she gives vocal classes to help others hear the
special music inside. She believes in the power of music and
story to shape and transform our world.

www.suncoastarts.com/paulinelebel.html

Chapter One

It was a sound. A sweet sound. High and light. And it twirled in the air like an acrobat turning somersaults. Then it tumbled down a waterfall, swam to shore and stretched out lazily on a sunny rock.

Aurora woke up suddenly. Another dream. Another dream of beautiful sound. And just in time for her birthday. It had been months since the last dream, and she'd worried that she might never have another one.

Then she heard it again. A real sound. She wasn't dreaming this time.

Aurora opened her eyes. All she saw in the darkness was the outline of the brick chimney at the foot of her bed. She knew the chimney would be cold by now. It would give her no warmth until mother went downstairs to light the kitchen stove for breakfast.

"Tibo," Aurora called gently. "Are you awake?"

But her younger brother, asleep on the other side of the chimney, did not stir in his bed.

Aurora reached under her pillow for the box of wooden matches. She struck one and lit the candle on her bedside table. She sat up and looked around the room. Everything was the same. The feather quilt, the washstand, the rag rugs making polka dots across the floor.

Then she heard the sound again. As lovely as the song a flower would sing. And she saw the window curtain billow like a sail.

"Is anyone there?" she whispered. But no one answered.

This was very strange. All her life, Aurora had wakened to silent mornings. No church bells ringing, no rooster crowing, nothing to announce the new day. In the peaceful land of Pindrop, noise was forbidden.

The curtain moved again.

She wrapped herself in the feather quilt, rolled out of bed and hobbled across the floor. A cold draft flowed from underneath the curtain. The window must have blown open during the night.

Aurora pulled the curtain aside and peered through the frosty windowpane. No sun yet. It was still hiding below the horizon. The only light came from the moon, hanging high in the sky like a lantern. She opened the window wider. An icy slap stung her face. Winter had arrived. There, in the moonlight, snowflakes glittered like frozen stars.

The sound was even closer now.

Aurora grabbed the edge of the windowsill and stuck her head out into the frozen morning as far as she could without falling over. She looked down to the ground and up to the sky and down to the ground again. The snow shining in the moonlight made the world seem clear and bright.

She saw the snow-dusted cobblestone streets and the leafless linden trees, their skeletal shapes like soldiers keeping watch. She saw the little pigs in their pen, huddled together for warmth. Wait. One ... two ... three ... one was missing. Her favorite, the one she had named Pepper.

Perhaps he was sniffing in the strawberry patch again, hoping to find a sweet red berry among the snow and dried leaves. Yes! There he was. And there was someone with him.

Aurora squinted. A stranger. An old woman with long hair as white as the snow. And, oh, how strangely she was dressed. Instead of the usual long cape of gray or brown wool, she wore a jumble of odd-colored shawls and skirts.

Over her shoulder she carried a worn leather pouch. In her right hand was a birdcage. The sound seemed to be coming from her direction.

What was she doing here? wondered Aurora. Perhaps she was one of those gypsy people who passed through selling pots and things.

Aurora watched in amazement as Pepper began to move. He lifted one leg up and down and then the others. He turned his body around in a circle as if he were dancing to the beautiful sound. Then the old woman stroked Pepper's head. Aurora thought she could see him smiling, a lopsided, piggy grin.

"Feathers," whispered Aurora. "She'd better not steal my pig."

The old woman turned, almost as if she had heard Aurora speak, and looked up at the window. Aurora caught her breath. A warm wave came over her, the kind you get when you step into a hot bath. She glowed from the top of her head right down to her toes. When she looked out again, Pepper was alone. The old woman was gone. And so was the beautiful sound.

Aurora shivered. She had no idea how long she had been standing there. She leaned out the window, but there was no sign of the old woman. Then she saw a figure walking away from the house. It was her father, Selmo the Whisperer. Was he off to the Whispering Hall for the morning service? It seemed much too early for that. Perhaps he, too, had heard the beautiful sound and had come outside to investigate.

Aurora closed the window quickly. It made no noise, for in the land of Pindrop, all windows were padded to dampen the sound. And the hinges were oiled every other week.

She shivered again, but this time from excitement. Ever since she could remember, she had heard sounds inside her head, lovely sounds that it seemed no one else in Pindrop heard. But this was the first time she had heard a beautiful sound on the outside. She danced lightly around the room and over to Tibo's bed.

"Get up, slug juice," said Aurora. "Today's my birthday."

Tibo yawned and pulled the quilt over his head. "Wake me up when it's time for the Sunwatch."

The Sunwatch was the most important holiday in Pindrop. It was a time to celebrate the winter solstice, the end of long, dark nights and the beginning of brighter, longer days leading to spring. Preparations for the big event had begun soon after the harvest, with the men carving wooden toys, and the women baking Sunwatch cookies and making long thin candles. Aurora had ten days of holiday from school. Ten days to herself, to go for long walks along the river and listen to the sounds in her head. There was really only one thing wrong with the Sunwatch: it showed up two days after Aurora's birthday, which meant everyone was too busy to pay much attention to her special day.

Aurora punched her fist into Tibo's quilt. He stuck out one hand and pinched her on the arm.

"Oooh," she moaned quietly, "I'm in danger for my life."

She walked to the washstand, poured water from a pitcher into the metal basin, splashed the cold water onto her face and wiped it dry with the hem of her flannelette nightshirt. Then she took down a Hush Cloth from the cupboard. Everyone in Pindrop wore Hush Cloths—small pieces of wool felt, held together with a leather thong—around their necks. That way, if they had to silence a cough or a sneeze, or needed to be especially quiet, they could simply lift the Hush Cloth over their mouths. "I think this is going to be my best birthday," said Aurora, adjusting the cloth below her chin. "My best birthday, ever."

AFTER A BREAKFAST of mashed turnip and sunflower seeds, Aurora helped her mother wash the dishes.

Megla the Dressmaker was a very tidy woman, the tidiest person Aurora had ever known. She never got stains on her woolen dresses or mud on her boots the way Aurora did. It seemed to Aurora that everything about her mother was perfect. Even her hair. Unlike Aurora's, which flew about her face as if it had a life of its own, her mother's hair was always tucked into a perfect circle at the back of her head like the pumpernickel dinner buns Panio the Baker made.

Sometimes Aurora sat in the kitchen and watched her mother while she sewed. She marveled at the small, even stitches and the way her mother cut the cloth smoothly and silently. Whenever Aurora tried to help with the cutting, she left ragged edges. And no matter how she held the scissors, they squeaked, which made her mother cross.

Megla did everything in silence, including the dishes. "The Silent Way is the best way," she always said. The dishpan was lined with sponges so that the dishes wouldn't rattle. The wet plates were stacked onto thick towels. And after the plates were dried, Aurora placed each one onto a quilted mat in the cupboard the way her mother had taught her.

But Aurora was not giving her full attention to the dishes. She was thinking of the beautiful sound and the strange old gypsy woman. Suddenly, she felt a large bowl slip from her hands. She caught it just before it landed on the floor. Megla didn't often get cross, but when she did, it usually had something to do with noise.

"I heard a very strange sound early this morning," said her mother, quietly.

"A sound?" Aurora blushed and placed the bowl very carefully into the cupboard.

"It was that pig of yours," Megla continued. "I'm sure of it. He wasn't properly trained in the first place. He'll have to go back and learn the Silent Way once and for all."

"Not Pepper. He's as quiet as a feather pillow. You must give him another chance."

"We'll see," said her mother. "I'll wait until after the holidays. Till then, do your best to shush him up. He listens to you. Now, take this to Lorio the Shopkeeper." Megla handed Aurora a shopping list. "And don't dawdle by the river. I have a lot of cleaning to do before the Sunwatch."

Aurora looked around the kitchen. Gleaming copper pots hung from the ceiling, the wood floor sparkled with beeswax and the large dining table had been scrubbed so often the wood was wearing away. She couldn't see anything that needed cleaning. Dust and crumbs didn't dare linger in her mother's kitchen.

Aurora sighed and walked into the cloakroom. She took down her cape from a hook, wrapped it around her shoulders and reached for her old brown boots. Then she remembered the new boots her aunt had sent her from Faraway. They were in a box in the corner. She lifted the lid. How wonderful. Red and shiny, with a small brass buckle at the ankle.

Hands trembling, she slipped on one red boot, then the other. Her feet had never looked more beautiful. She began to imagine the envious glances of the other children when her Mother interrupted her.

"I hope a certain young lady isn't thinking of wearing her new boots," she said from the kitchen. "They have to be brought to the shoemaker first for silencing. We can't have you clomping all over town."

Aurora's mother was right. It said so in the Hush Law.

Frilo the Magnificent, ruler of Pindrop, had ordered it: "All shoes and boots must be silenced with rubber soles -- at least two inches thick."

And yet ... it *was* her birthday. Would anyone notice that her boots hadn't been silenced if she walked very, very quietly? If she walked on tiptoe and scarcely put her feet down at all? Aurora decided they wouldn't.

Quickly, she stuffed her old brown boots into the box the new ones had come in. Then she tiptoed out the door, unaware that she was about to begin an adventure. An adventure that would forever change her life and the lives of everyone in the peaceful land of Pindrop.

CHAPTER TWO

"Where are you, Pepper?" Aurora called, keeping her voice low.

There in the snow were his small hoof prints, leading away from the strawberry patch. He had moved on when he found no breakfast there. And the cranberry bushes must also have been a disappointment. His curiosity had taken him farther a field. He was just the right size to squeeze between the fence boards and into the yard of their neighbor, Unso the Milkman.

Aurora climbed over the fence and started after him. She had completely forgotten about stepping lightly in her new boots. "Feathers!" she said as she watched Pepper heading straight for a can of goat's milk.

She reached him not a moment too soon and scooped up his wiggly body in her arms.

"Keep that pea-brained pig of yours away from my goats," said Unso the Milkman in a quiet but unfriendly voice.

Aurora turned and saw Unso bent over a wagon wheel. He was replacing the wheel silencers, thick leather strips that kept the metal wheels from clanking on the stony streets. She opened her mouth to defend Pepper, but the look on Unso's face silenced her. Unso was always mean at this time of year. Her mother said it had to do with the short, dreary days when the sun's light barely peeked over the horizon. And it seemed to Aurora that he was even meaner than last year. She carried Pepper over the fence and back to his pen.

"Oh, Pepper, mind your manners," said Aurora. "You're in enough trouble already." Pepper stuck his head through the wooden boards and nuzzled Aurora's knee. She smiled and scratched him behind the ears where he liked it best. Aurora didn't normally speak to animals, but Pepper was different. It seemed as if he understood what she was saying.

"It wasn't you who made that beautiful sound, was it?" she asked as she looked deep into Pepper's round, pink eyes. "You're a clever pig, but that didn't sound like a piggy noise to me."

Aurora decided she would ask Lorio the Shopkeeper. He was old and had seen many things. If anyone knew about the beautiful sound or the strange woman, it would be Lorio. She skipped along the road, admiring the trail made by her new boots in the snow. The morning was gray, and the pale sun offered no warmth. She wrapped her cape tight around her to keep out the chill.

She passed by a group of children silently rolling snowballs along the smooth surface of a frozen pond. She waved, but no one noticed her. They didn't even notice her red boots.

As she entered town, she saw Larch the Woodcutter. He was pushing a large wheelbarrow away from his wood wagon. She ran after him until she was close enough to speak without raising her voice. "Hello, Larch," she said, out of breath. "That's a heavy load."

"Quite right, Aurora," said Larch. "Quite right. Always the same this time of year. Everyone wants firewood for the Sunwatch. Why, I'm dead on my feet with all these deliveries. And so little daylight."

He stopped in front of a tall stone building, the majestic Whispering Hall. This was the place where everyone gathered to hear Aurora's father whisper the Tidings. Larch piled a huge load of firewood into his arms. He walked up the stairs, managing the first few steps nicely. Then something caused him to lose his footing and down he fell, pieces of wood sailing into the air and clattering noisily as they bounced down the stairs.

Aurora was about to go and help when she saw Larch shake his head. She looked up the stairs. Two men were standing at the front door. A tall one and a short one. They both wore the black capes of the Noise Police. Aurora's body became stiff with fear. The tall one was Nizzle, Captain of the Noise Police. She recognized his mustache—it looked like two centipedes about to meet beneath his nose. What would happen if he noticed that her boots hadn't been silenced? Aurora took a deep breath and commanded her feet to move. She dropped under Larch's wood wagon and waited.

"Arrest the noise doer, Sergeant Goth," Captain Nizzle said to the shorter man.

Sergeant Goth looked uncertain. "It was an accident," he said.

"Was that a noise I heard, Sergeant?"

Sergeant Goth nodded yes.

"And does this man have a noise permit?"

Sergeant Goth shook his head.

"Then the Law is clear," said Captain Nizzle. "Do your duty."

Goth looked at Larch sitting at the bottom of the stairs, rubbing his worried head where a log had hit him. "Perhaps a warning." Goth said.

This made Captain Nizzle angry. And whenever he got angry, he twisted his face, so the centipedes looked like they were about to pounce on each other.

"Remove this criminal from my sight and take him to the Quiet House. At once!" ordered Captain Nizzle. The centipedes were going wild.

Sergeant Goth snapped to attention and saluted. Stiffly, he walked down the stairs to Larch.

Aurora watched, horrified, as poor Larch was led away. She knew what they did to people at the Quiet House. The older children had told her. She decided to wait until Captain Nizzle went back into the Whispering Hall before moving from her hiding place. But first, a woman came out of the building carrying a small, crying baby. And because the baby was not wearing a Hush Cloth, the wailing could be heard for quite a distance.

Captain Nizzle stopped the woman with his arm. He reached into his hip pouch, pulled out a Hush Cloth and tied it around the baby's mouth. Aurora took in a sharp breath. She had been told about Captain Nizzle's Hush Cloths. They were made of the roughest, coarsest, scratchiest wool.

When there was silence again, Captain Nizzle went back inside. Aurora, her heart pounding, ran down the street past the stone buildings and the stony faces of the people who lived inside. At last she reached the main street of Pindrop. She stopped running and began to walk carefully on tiptoe among the silent, early morning shoppers. She kept her eyes on the wooden sidewalk, watching the plain brown shoes and boots pass her by. She decided not to stop in to see Panio the Baker for a poppy seed bun. It would be better to get her errands done and go right home.

She didn't feel safe until she was inside Lorio's General Store. She always felt safe there, with the dusty tin boxes of unknown treasures, the wooden barrels of dried fruits and nuts and the welcoming fire in the wood stove. Lorio the Shopkeeper stood behind the counter. No one else was in the store.

"They've taken Larch to the Quiet House," Aurora blurted.

Lorio looked up. "Poor man." He spoke in a hushed tone, the way everyone was expected to. "It's always like this. Near the holiday, I mean." He pulled his fingers through his gray hair -- what was left of it.

"And I'm wearing new boots. With no silencers. And I almost ran into Captain Nizzle."

"Oh, dear. You must walk very gently."

"It's not easy," said Aurora. And she handed him her mother's shopping list. Lorio put on his eyeglasses and examined the list carefully.

"I do have the broom. Yes, I do. Quite a nice corn broom at that. Excellent quality. Such a modern convenience. I'm sure your mother will like it."

"She wore out the last one."

"Yes," said Lorio. "If everyone used as many brooms as your mother, I'd be a wealthy man. But as for beeswax, well that's a different kettle of worms. I'm afraid I'm fresh out of beeswax until the new year. I suppose even the bees need a holiday."

Aurora smiled at his joke. But smiling was not encouraged in Pindrop because it can lead to giggling, and giggling can lead to laughing, and laughter, as everyone knows, is noisy. So Lorio became serious again. He moved his finger down the list, and when he got to the last item, the list began to shake. "I do have walnuts," he said. "Yes, walnuts are usually perfectly acceptable. But you see, oh, what a terrible mistake. I don't know how it happened. They brought me walnuts ... in the shell. And so, of course, the Noise Police won't allow me to sell them."

Aurora's eyes followed the shaking list. It fluttered so quickly, she could feel a breeze on her face.

"Well, you know what shells lead to," said Lorio.

Aurora shook her head. The only walnuts in the shell she had ever seen were high up in the old walnut tree by the creek. And children were not allowed to pick them. She had climbed it once and brought home a small, green thing, but it had shriveled into a stone at the back of her closet.

"Shells lead to cracking," said Lorio.

Aurora sighed. Everything always seemed to lead to something."

"The Noise Police are very fussy right now," he continued. "What with the holiday and all, they don't want anything to spoil the Sunwatch."

"Wouldn't it be lovely if something <u>did</u> spoil the Sunwatch," said Aurora. "Then I might have a proper birthday."

"Your birthday?" Lorio smiled. He opened a glass jar full of hard candies and presented one to Aurora.

"Blueberry, my favorite. Thanks," said Aurora, as she popped it into her mouth and sucked quietly.

"Lorio," she said, whispering, "I heard another beautiful sound this morning."

"Oh! Really?" His eyes grew wide. "How extraordinary."

"But this one was better than all the rest. I heard this one outside my head." Aurora paused for a moment, enjoying the look of astonishment on Lorio's face. "But you won't tell anyone, will you?"

"My lips are sealed," said Lorio.

"My mother thinks it was Pepper, but ..."

Just then the door opened. Aurora turned and saw Captain Nizzle's profile in the doorway. He was shaking his finger at someone. Captain Nizzle was famous for his keen ear. The older children said he could hear a person yawning three houses away. What if he'd heard Aurora talk about the beautiful sound? What if he'd noticed her boots and followed her to Lorio's store?

Before he could see her, she dashed around the counter to find safety behind a stack of dusty boxes. But the heel on her right boot got caught between two barrels. She dropped to the floor and grabbed her leg with both hands to twist it free.

Then she felt the floor vibrate as Captain Nizzle approached the counter, and she could hear the sound of Lorio's breathing coming in faster gulps.

"G-g-g-good and peaceful day to you, C-C-Captain Nizzle," said Lorio.

Captain Nizzle stopped at the edge of the counter. "I need your help with an urgent matter, Lorio," he said at last.

"A serious matter, you say?"

"Urgent," grunted Captain Nizzle.

"Well, that does sound ... urgent," said Lorio.

Captain Nizzle began to pace in front of the counter. Through the floorboards, Aurora could feel him moving toward her. She held her breath and hoped he wouldn't see the red boot sticking out from between the barrels. Then she heard Lorio lift the lid off the glass candy jar. Captain Nizzle turned abruptly and changed direction. She heard him remove a candy from the jar.

"Early this morning," said Captain Nizzle, "an old woman was seen entering the south gate into Pindrop. We have every reason to believe it is the Water World witch."

"Yes? Yes?" said Lorio.

"Zantalalia," said Captain Nizzle.

"No. No," said Lorio.

"Yes, yes," said Captain Nizzle. "Zantalalia. That old crazy woman."

"Are you sure?" asked Lorio. "It's been years ... People change."

"Sooner or later she will come to your shop to buy supplies. She must be stopped. Nothing, I repeat, nothing must disturb the silence of the Sunwatch."

Suddenly, there was a small crunching sound. Captain Nizzle had accidentally bitten down on the hard candy.

"You're selling rather noisy candy this year, Lorio."

"The s-s-sign on the jar says for s-s-sucking only, Captain."

"I *was* sucking, Lorio," said Captain Nizzle. "I'm afraid you give me no other option. I'll have to confiscate the entire jar. Who knows what could happen if a gang of children got hold of these."

Aurora heard the precious jar move across the counter. Captain Nizzle turned to go. And as he did, his long black cape fluttered over the counter, launching tiny balloons of dust into the air. They floated over the barrels of nuts and raisins and sailed toward Aurora. One made a perfect landing right inside her nose. She felt that familiar tickle, Oh, no! She mustn't sneeze! She tried to reach for her Hush Cloth, but she was too late. GZPKLT!

"What was that?" asked Captain Nizzle, turning to look at Lorio.

Lorio sniffled and spoke in a husky voice. "I—I—I think I might have a touch of the f-f-flu," and he pressed his Hush Cloth to his nose.

"Take care of it, Lorio," said Captain Nizzle as he walked out the door. "We wouldn't want anything to happen to you." But his voice sounded most insincere.

When Captain Nizzle had gone, Lorio helped Aurora get up from her hiding place. He was trembling like an aspen in a storm.

"I'm sorry," said Aurora. "I couldn't stop it. It happened so suddenly."

"Don't worry," he said.

Aurora shook the dust from her cape.

"And now, Aurora, you must go home."

"But who is this Zanta ...?"

"Zanta–lalia," said Lorio. "A voice, a radiant voice, brighter than a thousand suns."

Aurora watched Lorio's face. His eyes were open, but he seemed to be dreaming.

"Then why did they send her to the Water World?" she asked.

"She made noise," said Lorio. "It was her calling."

"Her calling?"

"Her gift."

"What kind of noise did she make?"

"The most wonderful noise," Lorio answered dreamily.

Then his reverie ended and he began to tremble again. "Now really, Aurora, you must go."

Aurora left the store with the corn broom in hand, her thoughts full of the voice brighter than a thousand suns. She had taken only a few steps when one beautiful red boot with a small brass buckle at the ankle made a creaking sound. Just a tiny sound at first. But it got louder with each step. She looked down at her right boot. The leather heel was flapping. It must have ripped when it got caught between the barrels.

Someone looked over a fence, and a pair of eyes scolded her. She hopped on her left foot, using the broom as a crutch. But because there were no rubber silencers on her boots, that made even more noise. A woman walked by. "Hush, child," she said. Soon Aurora was surrounded by shaking heads and wagging fingers. Perhaps the best thing to do was to remove the boots and walk in her socks.

Through a small gap in the crowd, Aurora caught a

glimpse of a black chariot pulled by a black horse. Standing inside the chariot was none other than Captain Nizzle. He held a large ear horn to his ear, and his mouth was curled up in distaste as if he had seen a beetle swimming in his breakfast porridge.

Aurora ran quickly down a side street, her boot squeaking loudly. Nizzle gave a smart crack with his whip. "Onward, Whist," he commanded, and the horse bounded in the direction of Aurora's noisy boot.

Aurora looked behind to see if the chariot was gaining on her, and she ran right into a wooden fence. It was too high to climb over. She turned and saw an old granary, the windows covered over with dirt. She ran to the door. A padlock was fastened to it. She hurried around to the side of the building, hoping to find an open window. The grasses had grown tall, making it hard to run.

Suddenly, her feet fell from under her. She shot straight down like an arrow, and the earth swallowed her up.

CHAPTER THREE

Aurora sat in the dark in a place that smelled like rotting turnips. She had heard a cracking sound as she went down, and something on her face felt like dirt. She was in some sort of root cellar. The old cellar door must have given way under her weight, for she had plunged through and landed on a hard shelf. From above, she heard the muted sound of the chariot wheels. Would Captain Nizzle see the hole? Or would the tall grasses cover the opening? The wheels came closer and closer. Then they moved on. Aurora was safe from Captain Nizzle— for now.

Only a narrow shaft of light streamed down the hole as Aurora wiggled her hips to get off the shelf. She stopped suddenly. Something had touched her. It felt like fingers. Long, spiny fingers. And lots of them. They poked at her again. She gasped. Her hand landed on a hard object. It was the broom. She picked it up and began to beat at her attackers. Something fell to the floor. Squinting in the dim light, she saw that they were only potatoes, old potatoes sprouting long, white potato fingers. She sighed with relief and jumped down from the shelf.

Aurora could see no windows in the cellar, and the hole in the door was too high to reach. She would have to find some other way out of this place.

She took a small, cautious step, holding the broom in front of her. Toe, heel. Her boot didn't squeak. Another cautious step. And another. Then she noticed that the heel on her right boot was missing. It must have come off during the fall. Her beautiful new boots ruined already.

She came to a stairway and climbed the rickety steps. Now she was in a spacious room. This one had windows, but they were so caked with dirt that only meager light filtered through. Scattered about the room were odd, white shapes. She was about to reach out to touch one when she sensed she was not alone. Someone or something moved in the shadows.

She backed up too quickly on her wobbly shoe and lost her balance. As she went down, she struck something that looked like a large hat box. It made a sound like thunder. Aurora was struck with terror. She put her hands over her ears.

A candle flickered in the corner as a shadow moved into the light. Aurora looked up and recognized the layers of shawls and skirts she had seen that morning outside her bedroom window. Now, up close, the colors dazzled her—bright yellow and orange and purple and green—colors Aurora had seen only in her paint box. It was the old gypsy woman.

Her hair was wild about her face, a brown face with deep cracks, like the ground last summer when it hadn't rained for two months. Aurora reached for her broom, but the old woman moved quickly and stamped her foot on it. "Speak up, child. Who sent you here?"

Aurora was confused. "Well, no one really. You see... Captain Nizzle..."

"Captain Nizzle!" the old woman said. "Who's Captain Nizzle?"

"He's the Captain of the Noise Police," Aurora answered.

"The Captain of the Noise Police sent you?"

"No," said Aurora. "My boot was squeaking, and he was chasing after me and..." And Aurora started to cry, which made her feel very foolish. She was not the kind of person who burst into tears. It was just that so many things had happened already this morning—so many strange and wonderful and terrible things.

The old woman moved toward her. Aurora pulled back quickly in fright, and as she did she struck the box again. She covered her ears and cried even harder.

"It's all right," said the old woman. "Everything is all right. You just fell on a drum."

Aurora had no idea what she was talking about. A drum? "And it was the finest drumming I've heard in years. Come now, child, get up." She offered her hand to Aurora, but Aurora shook her head and used the broom to help herself up.

"What is this place?" she asked, regaining her composure and dusting herself off.

"This is the past," said the old woman, making a wide gesture with the candle around the gloomy room. "And the future, if I have anything to say about it," she added in a mysterious voice.

"Are you the lady from the Water World?"

"I am Zantalalia." The old woman bent gracefully into a curtsy.

"And I am Aurora," said Aurora, imitating her curtsy.

"I know," said Zantalalia. "I'd recognize those eyes anywhere. You're old Jessup's granddaughter."

Aurora shook her head. "I don't think so. I don't know any Jessup."

"Of course not. How could you know about the past when they go around locking everything up?" Zantalalia walked over to one of the white stacks.

"What are these things?" asked Aurora.

"Your inheritance," answered Zantalalia. And with a grand gesture, she swept away a white cloth. Dust filled the air. Aurora sneezed. Once. Twice. The second time even louder than the first. Zantalalia didn't seem to mind the noise, so Aurora didn't bother to pull on her Hush Cloth.

Aurora gazed at the pile of strange things, big and small wooden things with strings stretched across them. Zantalalia picked one up and plucked the strings. It made an enchanting sound that reminded Aurora of a stream in springtime as it tripped over stones.

"Thank heavens," said Zantalalia. "My fiddles...they're safe. Dusty and moldy. But safe."

"Your...fiddles?" asked Aurora. "But what are they doing here?"

"The Noise Police brought them. After the Hush Law was passed."

"You mean it used to be noisy here?"

"Joyfully noisy."

"And people didn't whisper?"

"Only when they shared a secret."

"But why did you let them take your fiddles? Didn't anyone try to stop them?"

Zantalalia put the fiddle down. "At first. But the Noise Police were very persistent, and they had their informers. Soon everyone was too afraid. Afraid of a knock at the door. Of footsteps in the night. Afraid of each other."

Zantalalia walked over to another stack. Aurora watched as the old woman folded back the white cloth very gently so as not to stir up the dust. Underneath was a tangle of bright brass tubes, all twisted together.

"Do all these things make noise?" asked Aurora, inching closer to have a look.

Zantalalia smiled, and when she did, her face didn't seem quite so terrifying. "I call it music," she said. She picked up a brass pipe that was open at one end like a laughing mouth. She put the small end to her lips and blew into it. It made a bright sound. "This was your grandfather's bugle," the old woman said. "And that horn, as well. He made such beautiful music."

Aurora was confused. How could this be? No one had ever talked about her grandfather before. "I don't believe you," she said.

Zantalalia reached into her pocket and took out a silver key. It seemed to glow in the dim light. And as Aurora held it, her hand grew warm.

"Is it magic?" she asked, wondering how much hotter it might get.

"Yes, I suppose it is."

"I don't believe in magic," said Aurora.

"That's all right. Even if you don't believe in it, the magic still works."

"What kind of magic does it do?"

"One magic thing," said Zantalalia. "Whoever holds the key will speak the truth."

Aurora examined the key carefully. "Captain Nizzle said you were an old crazy woman."

"Hah!" said Zantalalia. "What else would you expect from the Noise Police! But you, child, what do you think?"

Aurora clutched the key tightly in her hand, trying to wring the truth from it. She felt her hand get very hot, and she heard herself saying, "I think you're a wise old crazy woman."

Zantalalia laughed. "Well, perhaps that is the truth. But only part of it. I have many more truths to share with you, Aurora, if you'll come to my cabin in the forest this afternoon."

Aurora was unsure. She knew that her parents would forbid her to go. But they would also have forbidden her to wear her new boots, and then she would never have known about the noise makers in the old granary. It was time she started thinking for herself. She wanted to learn more about the beautiful noises, and this old woman could teach her. Aurora looked up at the stranger and saw a kind gentle beautiful face behind the wrinkles. She nodded her head yes.

With the corn broom, Zantalalia drew a map in the dusty floor. "Follow the path along Laughing Creek …"

"Laughing Creek?" interrupted Aurora. "We call it Crazy Creek."

"Humph," said Zantalalia and continued. "As I was saying, take the path along Laughing Creek to the mouth of the River of Joy."

Aurora decided not to interrupt again. But no one in Pindrop called it the River of Joy. Everyone knew it was the River of Sorrow.

"Walk along the river seventy-five steps. No, wait. You've got small feet. Better make it a hundred. Then turn and go up the hill into the forest. The path to the cabin begins where the two chestnut trees meet."

"I'll find it," said Aurora.

"Bring the key with you. And remember to come alone."

Zantalalia erased the map with the broom and returned it to Aurora. "I think we can find you an easier way out," she said as she led her to a narrow door. Then her face became serious. "Do they still celebrate the Sunwatch here?"

"Yes," said Aurora.

"Good. Then I'm not too late." She opened the door and stuck her head out. It was the backyard of the granary. No one was around. "Go," she said.

Aurora walked out the door, dragging the broom behind her in the snow, so it would cover up her footprints. Just in case.

THE FIRST THING Aurora did when she got home was to take off her new boots. They certainly didn't look new and shiny anymore. And there was a rough edge where the heel had ripped off. She put the boots back in the box and stuck them far into the corner, hoping her mother would forget about them. Then she walked into the kitchen and propped the broom against the counter. Her mother was so busy she might not notice that the ends were a bit ragged.

"No beeswax?" said her mother, shining a copper pot. "That means I won't be able to polish the tables."

"Not until the new year," said Aurora. "And no walnuts either."

"Oh, no," said Megla.

"They arrived with the shells on."

"Oh, well. At least it's good to know the Noise Police are doing their job." She continued to rub the cloth over the shiny pot in small, even circles. Then she stopped and looked up from her work. "Would you like to invite someone for your birthday?"

Aurora shrugged her shoulders.

"What about the girl you were playing with last week?"

"She's just like the others," said Aurora. "She thinks I'm crazy because I hear sounds."

Megla's face flushed. "Aurora! I have forbidden you to speak about that."

"But the sounds are so beautiful," said Aurora. "Why wouldn't everyone want to hear about them?"

"It's bothersome to others," said her mother sharply.

"But how can it bother anyone if the noise is inside my head?"

"Mind your tongue," said Megla. Then her voice softened a bit. "Go and see your father. It's time for your whispering lesson."

Aurora always looked forward to her whispering lessons. Not because she enjoyed the whispering so much, but it meant she could sit in her father's study. Just like one of the grownups. And if he was pleased with her work, he might let her sit at his desk and read from one of the many books in the bookcase that reached to the ceiling.

"I hope you're in good whisper today," said Selmo the Whisperer.

Aurora smiled and went to the bookcase. She took down two identical bowls, one smaller than the other, and gave the large bowl to her father. She had done this every day for the past year, but today it didn't feel the same.

"What is the first thing you have to remember?" asked Selmo.

"To keep a firm grip on the Whispering Bowl," said Aurora, gripping the bowl tightly.

"That's right," said Selmo. "Now relax your shoulders. Open your throat. And let the air rush out of you like the wind." Selmo made a small sound like the wind blowing gently through the trees. Aurora did the same. *Whoosh!*

"Fine," said Selmo. "Now let's begin." And in a dark, throaty whisper that could be heard across the room, he spoke over the Whispering Bowl. "May your steps be as silent as the shadows."

Aurora held the Whispering Bowl, took a deep breath and answered in the same dark whisper. "And may your words be as light as the dew." She heard her voice tremble.

Her father continued. "Today in the silent land of Pindrop, these are the Tidings." He looked at Aurora and waited.

Aurora took another deep breath. Such a deep breath that she choked and coughed.

Selmo looked at her in concern. "Are you ill, Aurora?"

"No, Father."

"Is something troubling you then?"

Yes, she wanted to say, yes, something is troubling me.

Everything is troubling me. Hat boxes in an old granary that make a sound like thunder, and an old woman who doesn't wear a Hush Cloth and likes to make beautiful noise, and brass things that belong to a grandfather that no one has told me about. She wanted to ask about all these things, but she knew it would make her father angry. And she didn't want anything to spoil her birthday.

"What is it, Aurora? Have you been hearing sounds again?"

She hesitated. "Yes, Father. In my dreams," she added quickly. "And I saw something. A long brass tube that made a fat noise. And there was a wooden box with strings on it, and they made a tinkling sound when they were touched. What are these things, Father?"

Selmo's face became serious. "It's just your imagination, Aurora." He took Aurora's hand. "But don't worry, dear. When you grow up and understand the Pindrop way, you won't be bothered by those sounds anymore."

Aurora was shocked. "I won't?"

"I'm sure of it," said Selmo.

Aurora felt dismayed. She didn't want to stop hearing the sounds. Ever. They were as important to her as breathing.

Chapter Four

"Where you going?" asked Tibo.

Aurora had shut the back door as quietly as possible. She had inched her way along the side of the house, one step at a time. But her younger brother had the eyes of an eagle. He was playing that strange game of his, collecting lengths of twine and yarn, and winding them round and round to make a ball. The curious thing was, no matter how much string he added, the ball never seemed to get any bigger.

"None of your business," said Aurora as she walked toward him. Tibo tugged at a burlap sack that covered Megla's rosebush, hoping to add one of the strings to his ball. Aurora could see he wasn't having any success, so she reached over and grabbed a loose thread. She yanked it hard, but it was quite strong. At last it let go, and she handed Tibo a long thread.

"Goodie," said Tibo. "But where you going?"

"For a walk," said Aurora, trying to make it sound unimportant.

"Me, too," grinned Tibo.

"No," said Aurora. "I'm going by myself."

"Then why've you got your fancy clothes on?"

Aurora frowned. "It's my birthday, in case you forgot."

"But I have no one to play with."

"Don't be such a jellyfish," said Aurora running off. "I'll play with you when I get back. And look after Pepper while I'm gone."

AURORA FOLLOWED Zantalalia's instructions to the letter. She knew the path along the creek. She often sat there and listened to the sounds in her head. This time she listened closely to the water bubbling over the stones, and she began to understand why the old woman had called it the Laughing Creek. It made a low, rippling sound, almost a chuckle. In the springtime, she thought, when the water rushed down from the mountain and swelled the banks, it must burst out laughing.

As she reached the mouth of the River of Sorrow, she remembered that the old woman had called it the River of Joy. Could laughing lead to joy? she wondered.

She counted off one hundred steps and began to walk up the hill. It was early afternoon, but the sun hovered weakly, not strong enough to melt the snow that had fallen that morning.

At the top of the hill, Aurora had the strange feeling that someone was following her. She stepped behind a large rock and poked her head out, just enough to see Tibo. He was struggling up the hill on his short little legs, still clutching the ball of string in his hand.

He's become far too nosy for his own good, thought Aurora. She would have to teach him a lesson. She dropped back behind the rock and tried to remember what her father had taught her. She had no Whispering Bowl, so she cupped her hands under her mouth. She opened her throat and let the air rush out of her like the wind, and in a dark mysterious voice, she whispered, "Today in the land of Pindrop, a foolish young boy entered the dangerous forest and was swallowed alive by the evil jillyjum tree."

Aurora heard a tiny shriek, and when she looked out from behind the rock, she saw Tibo running straight down the hill. He was running so fast that he dropped his string ball. It rolled slowly down the hill, picking up snow as it went, turning into a large snowball before it stopped behind a rock.

Aurora watched Tibo run out of sight. Then she turned to enter the forest. There she saw a skunk waddling down the hill, sniffing at the snow. Was this the real cause of

Tibo's fright? Aurora stood very still until the skunk had disappeared into the bushes by the river. Then she walked down the hill to rescue Tibo's string ball. She had never liked the thing very much—all those bits and pieces gathered from who knows where. He had started collecting them when his rabbit died. Mother had never scolded him about it, perhaps because it didn't make any noise. She brushed the snow off the string ball and thought about where to put it. She had a clean handkerchief in her right pocket and raisins in her left. She decided to stuff it behind the large rock and pick it up on her way back.

Aurora searched along the edge of the forest for the spot the old woman had talked about, where the two chestnut trees meet. At last she saw them. Two towering trees, almost the same height, their branches like twisted fingers joined together to form an archway. Aurora passed under it and entered the dark, still world of the forest.

The path had not been used for many years. It was covered with bramble bushes and tree roots that poked out of the thin carpet of snow. She moved slowly, carefully, but her cape caught on a bush. Aurora jerked herself away and landed against the rough bark of a large tree. She found the path again and moved on, stubbing her toes on the roots. The farther she walked, the darker it became.

What if the story she had made up was really true? What if there really was a jillyjum tree that swallowed up children? She was in the middle of giving herself a good scare when she noticed it was getting brighter. At the end of the path was a clearing. And in the clearing stood an old cabin. It had weathered over the years and it leaned so badly to one side that it looked as if it might topple at any moment. The roof was dressed in bright green moss sprinkled with snow, and a stork's nest sat like a hat on top of the chimney. Aurora heard a beautiful sound, like the sounds in her dreams, but with words in a strange language. Was this Zantalalia's music? Was this the voice brighter than a thousand suns?

The sound, like a magnet, drew her around to the back of the cabin. She saw a large yard closed in by a sprawling fence, with bushes growing through the fence boards. Stacks of rusted tools were scattered about a garden that had long ago been reclaimed by weeds. And in the center stood Zantalalia wearing the paint-box colors. She stabbed at the hard ground with a spade and scooped out small amounts of dirt. She stopped singing, suddenly, then turned and saw Aurora.

"Well, don't just stand there like a stork," she said. "Grab a spade and help me."

Aurora picked up a spade from the ground. It was heavy and dirty. She began to dig. The cold wind stung her back. She had no idea what they were digging for, and Zantalalia didn't bother to explain. They dug side by side in the faint winter light. Aurora was tired and thirsty and ready to quit when her shovel struck wood.

"Easy now," said Zantalalia. "We don't want to damage anything."

Aurora peered into the hole. Inside was a wooden box the size of a small toy chest. They lifted it carefully out of the ground and carried it into Zantalalia's cabin, which was really just one large room. On the kitchen table was a birdcage, the same birdcage that Zantalalia had been carrying when Aurora had seen her that morning. It was big and shiny and empty. They set the box down beside it.

Zantalalia stoked the fire in the wood stove. She ladled water from a rusty pail into a copper tea kettle and put the kettle to boil on the stove. Unlike Aurora's quiet house, this one wasn't padded and oiled according to the Hush Law. The cupboard door squeaked when it was shut, the kettle clanked when it was placed on the stove, and Zantalalia tapped the floor as she walked about in her boots with no rubber soles. Aurora found these noises unpleasant. But she did enjoy the sound of the old woman's necklace. Instead of a Hush Cloth, Zantalalia wore a necklace of turquoise and pink seashells, and the shells jingled with every step she took.

Aurora turned to hang her cape on a hook by the door. She stopped at an elaborate spider web dangling from the ceiling.

"You mustn't disturb her spinning," said Zantalalia. "It's more her home now than mine."

How strange, thought Aurora. Megla would never let a spider take over her kitchen. She looked around the dusty room and decided to lay her cape over the back of a chair.

Meanwhile, Zantalalia picked up the wooden box, and with a knife she sliced through the wax that sealed the edges. Then she pulled off the lid and lifted out the most wonderful thing Aurora had ever seen. It looked like a large, round serving dish with a domed lid. Not just any ordinary serving dish, but the kind used for only the most important occasion. The surface was polished gold, and on the side was a painted bird with a black face and white beak. His long turquoise feathers glistened with jewels. A circle of golden knobs crowned the top of the dome, and at the base was an inscription: *For my dearest Zantalalia.*

"A present!" said Aurora. "Who gave it to you?"

"A man," said Zantalalia. "A man I loved very much. Such a long time ago." Then she asked sharply, "Did you bring the key?"

Aurora was surprised. She wondered what other magic the key might do. She took the silver key from her pocket and gave it to Zantalalia. "What is this thing?" she asked turning her gaze again to the mysterious present from long ago.

"A Song Spinner," answered Zantalalia.

"A Song Spinner?"

"A music machine."

Aurora still didn't understand.

"Listen."

Aurora's eyes glowed with excitement as she watched the old woman place the magic key into the top of the Song Spinner. Zantalalia twisted the key to the left. Once, twice, three times. She removed the key, grabbed hold of one of the gold knobs at the top and pulled. Slowly, the Song Spinner began to turn on its base, round and round. Soon the carved bird was spinning so fast that all Aurora could see were the brilliant feathers flashing in front of her eyes.

The room filled with sound. Aurora had never heard so many lovely sounds—deep ones, high ones, sweet ones, loud and soft ones. It was as if all the sounds she had ever heard inside her head had decided to come out and play together. She began to laugh and to weep at the same time, her body swaying to the music.

"I knew it had to be real," she said. "Not just my imagination."

Zantalalia smiled, and Aurora could see that many years ago she would have been a beautiful young woman. "You like it?" she asked.

"Oh, yes," said Aurora. "It's the most wonderful noise I ever heard. Even better than the sounds in my head."

Zantalalia took Aurora's hands and danced her around the room. She had never danced before. Not like this. The old woman spun her about and showed her how to kick her legs high into the air. Aurora tapped and twirled while Zantalalia picked up two metal spoons and slapped them in time to the music. Then the old woman spoke to the birdcage on the table. "Sounds as good as new doesn't it, Doremi?"

Aurora stopped twirling. She looked at the birdcage. It was empty. Zantalalia had spoken to an empty birdcage. Was the old woman crazy after all?

CHAPTER FIVE

As this strangest of afternoons wore on, Aurora learned more about the Song Spinner and Zantalalia's secret past.

"One night," said Zantalalia, "the Noise Police came to my door. They took my musical things. My drums, my flutes. Isn't that right, Doremi?" She looked at the birdcage and sighed.

Aurora turned and squinted. How she wished she could see something. But all she saw was an empty birdcage.

"Everything except the Song Spinner," continued the old woman. "The fools. They must have thought it was a serving dish," she chuckled. "So I buried it that night. And the next morning they sent us to the Water World."

"The Water World is a terrible place full of terrible people," said Aurora.

"Have you been there?"

"Why, no," answered Aurora. "But my mother told me."

"Your mother? I don't suppose your mother has been there either. And such a fine lady she must be, dressing you in all these fine things. My mother was only a gypsy woman. But she taught me never to pass judgment on people and places I'd never seen."

"I'm sorry. I won't do it again." Aurora looked down at her lap, and with the back of her hand, she stroked the smooth woolen skirt her mother had made her. "This is my best skirt. It's my birthday today."

"Ah, yes, your birthday," said the old woman, her eyes huge and round inside her wrinkled face, like buttons in a cushion, "How wonderful. Why, it's been years since I've had call to sing the birthday song. Let's see ... now, how does it go?" She tapped her chin with one finger to help her remember. "Ta-ra-ra ... no, that's not it ... Tee-dum-dum-dum ... no, no."

"Is it a happy song?"

"Oh, very," said Zantalalia, and then she had it.

"*Dyessa, dyessa joont,* Au-ro-ra," the old woman sang in a sunny voice. "*Dyessa al-ma-ta joont.*"

Aurora guessed she must be singing in the Water World language. She smiled. It was the first time anyone had sung her a birthday song. She was delighted, even if she didn't understand the words.

Zantalalia looked toward the birdcage. "And Doremi says he wishes you many more birthdays to come." She took a few sunflower seeds from one of her many pockets and placed them in the cage. Aurora looked at the birdcage again. Except for the seeds, it was most definitely empty.

"Zantalalia," asked Aurora shyly. "Why do you talk to an empty birdcage?"

"Empty!" said Zantalalia. "Empty? Doremi, this little snippet thinks your birdcage is empty!"

Aurora felt terrible. She hadn't meant to offend anyone.

"What's that, Doremi?" asked Zantalalia. "Oh, dear me. Of course." She reached into another pocket and took out a square canvas bag tied up with a leather thong. She opened it very carefully and removed a small piece of rice paper, painted with vibrant colors. She looked at the painting and pressed it to her heart. "Once upon a time," she said, "a beautiful bird lived in this cage. A beautiful singing bird named Do-re-mi."

"A bird that sings?"

"Before the evil Hush Law, there were many singing birds. Everything was allowed to be what it was. A bird was a singer and a cow was a mooer and a pig was an oinker."

"My pig, Pepper, is going to be sent away to a special school because my mother thinks he makes too much noise."

"What nonsense, sending pigs to school. And I'm sure what they do to keep them quiet isn't very pretty."

Aurora thought about Pepper. If they made him wear a Hush Cloth, he wouldn't be able to root around for strawberries.

She decided she would never let him go.

Zantalalia held up the rice paper painting for Aurora to see. She could tell it was old because the edges had yellowed. But it was still beautiful. And extraordinary. Even though it was a small painting, you could see a crowd of people, all with rosy cheeks and pink lips. They were in some sort of hall, blazing with light and color, decorated with holly and ivy. So many people—all smiling—as if they never worried at all about making noise.

"What's going on here?" asked Aurora.

"Can't you see?"

"No. There are too many people crowded together."

"Then try to imagine what would be happening. Look very closely and try to imagine what everyone is doing."

Aurora looked deep into the painting, into the sea of people. She kept looking until at last the painting seemed to come alive.

On the stage was a beautiful woman. She was singing with a large colorful bird perched on her shoulder. And dancers in golden costumes were swaying across the floor.

Aurora looked more closely. Something about this place was familiar. The long curtains were blue. And the stained glass windows showed the seasons—winter, spring, summer, fall.

"It looks like the Whispering Hall in Pindrop," said Aurora.

"Whispering Hall. What nonsense!" said Zantalalia. "No one had to whisper then. There was singing and dancing and so much joy. And in those days, Pindrop was called Shandrilan."

"Shandrilan," Aurora repeated, enjoying the taste of the word. "And who is that beautiful lady?"

Zantalalia laughed. "Why, that's me."

"And the bird on your shoulder. That must be Doremi."

"Yes. Such a splendid voice. Doremi and I sang duets for all the great Kings and Queens. In fact, it was Queen Althea of Balatania who gave him to me. And I taught him all the songs."

Zantalalia pointed to a man blowing into a long brass pipe. "That's your Grandfather Jessup playing the horn," she said.

Suddenly, there was a loud shriek. Aurora put her hands over her ears, terrified. "It's the tea kettle," said Zantalalia, getting up.

Aurora had never heard anything so harsh. It felt as if a pin were being pushed into her ear. She had thought that all sound would be beautiful. But it seemed a few would take some getting used to.

"Isn't it a lovely kettle?" asked Zantalalia. "A gift from the King of Sumeria." But Aurora wasn't at all sure that a lovely thing should make such a racket.

Zantalalia took the kettle from the heat and poured the boiling water into a teapot. "Life was rip-roaring then," she said. "People could be *fortissimo*. That means good and loud. Not like today. Always *pianissimo*," she hissed quietly.

She put the kettle down. "Of course, sometimes things got a little carried away, overjubilant, you might say. And there were those who used loud words to quarrel with their neighbors. But then people can be just as mean in whispers."

Aurora remembered ornery Unso the Milkman and knew instantly what Zantalalia meant. She looked again at the rice paper painting. "What about my grandfather?"

"He was sent to the Water World like the rest of us," answered Zantalalia.

Aurora's heart sank. She didn't want to believe this. She hoped he would have been spared.

"Such a fine musician. I'm sure you inherited his talent."

"But where is he?" Aurora wanted to know.

Zantalalia's eyes became cloudy. "Poor old Jessup," she said. "He was never very strong. He caught pneumonia last spring. It was the dampness. Winters are very damp in the Water World. Not even the best of my herbs could save him."

Aurora dropped her head sadly. "And I never knew him."

"Oh, but you did," said Zantalalia, trying to sound cheerful. "You see, there was a neighbor of yours who used to come to the Water World every fall to cut reeds. He told us that Jessup had a brand new granddaughter. So Jessup stowed away on a boat and jumped overboard near Pindrop. He hid in your father's pig barn during the day, and when he was certain everyone was asleep, he climbed up into your room. He held you in his arms and rocked you, and sang softly. All the old songs. He often told me how you smiled at him. When he got back, he never stopped talking about you."

As Aurora's eyes filled with tears, Zantalalia took her in her arms and held her close.

Aurora tried hard to remember. To let herself go back to the time when she was a baby. To hear the songs of her grandfather again. "The sounds in my head," she said, beginning to understand. "He was the one who put them there." She reached into her pocket for a handkerchief and blew her nose. Loudly. "I wish he had stayed."

"Too dangerous," said Zantalalia. "For Jessup and for your family." Zantalalia poured the tea and handed Aurora a bowl of something dark and mysterious. Aurora took a small brave sip. She had never tasted anything so good—spicy and sweet.

"Zantalalia," she asked, "do you hear sounds in your head?"

"Of course. All the time. Why, there's music in everything."

Aurora picked up a polished stone from the table. "Even in this?"

"You only have to know how to listen," said Zantalalia.

Aurora put the stone to her ear and listened. Perhaps one day she would be able to hear something.

"There's music everywhere you look," said Zantalalia. And she began to make all kinds of sounds with her voice. The sound of a tree rustling in the breeze, the sound of a horse galloping without padded boots, the sound of a bee searching for clover. It seemed she could do anything with her voice. Then she buzzed like a mosquito, a loud whining sound, the kind you hear after you've turned out the light, gotten into bed and are just about to fall asleep.

Now, Aurora knew that Zantalalia was making the sound, and she also knew that she had never seen a mosquito in winter, but the sound was so real she couldn't stop her eyes from darting around the room. Then she felt a mosquito land on her arm— she was sure of it. She smacked it as hard as she could. But when she lifted her hand, nothing was there.

They both had a good laugh over that.

"The songs are still everywhere," said Zantalalia. "If only the people would learn to sing them again."

"I will learn to sing them," said Aurora.

"Good," said Zantalalia, smiling.

"And Doremi? Does he still sing?"

"My poor Doremi. He wasn't meant for life in the Water World. It broke his heart. He went to sleep one night and never woke up."

Aurora looked at the birdcage sadly.

"I couldn't part with his cage," said Zantalalia. "It's company. Someone to talk to in my old years. And, you know, when you walk around with an empty birdcage and carry on a conversation with an invisible bird, people don't bother you much."

Their laughter was cut short by a knock at the door. Aurora froze in fear. Door knocking was strictly forbidden by the Hush Law. "Did you tell anyone you were coming?" whispered Zantalalia. "No one," said Aurora, in her tiniest voice.

Zantalalia grabbed Aurora's cape off the back of the chair and pushed it into her arms. She walked quickly to a rug on the floor and pulled it aside. Underneath was a small door that led to a cellar. "Stay in there until I come for you," she said, opening the door.

Aurora climbed down the steep ladder. When the cellar door was shut, a musty darkness closed in around her.

Chapter Six

I t was pitch black in the cellar. And cold, too. Aurora
wrapped the cape around her shoulders and listened
to the sounds above. First, she heard Zantalalia's
boots walking to the door, then a very excited voice.
But she couldn't make out the speaker or the words.

She moved lightly up the ladder and pushed the cellar
door open. Just a crack. It was Lorio the Shopkeeper! His
face was very pale, and he spoke in quick bursts, his hands
swaying from side to side as if he were shooing flies.

"He was in my store twice today," Lorio said. "Please be
careful."

He held out a large sack for Zantalalia. She opened it
and took out a loaf of bread, a circle of cheese, and potatoes,
beets and onions. "Thank you, dear friend," she said as she
placed the food on the counter.

Then Zantalalia put her arms around Lorio and held
him.

When he was gone, Aurora pushed the cellar door open
and crawled out.

"What did Lorio want? Why did he come here?"

"To bring me news," said Zantalalia. "And I'm afraid it
isn't good. I'll have to change my plans."

Zantalalia crossed her arms and walked around the
kitchen table, looking up and squinting as if she was trying
to read something written on the ceiling. Then she stopped
by the Song Spinner and placed her hand over the bird with
the turquoise feathers the way you would pet a favorite cat.

"The Song Spinner," she said very slowly, "belongs to
you."

Aurora gasped. "But it's yours!"

"It was promised to you before your grandfather died," said Zantalalia." He was thin and frail but strong enough to speak to me. Quite delirious, he was, mixing up the past with the present. But about one thing he was very clear. He wanted me to return to Pindrop and find you. On your birthday. I told him it wasn't a good idea. I couldn't think of many people who would be tickled pink to see me again."

Zantalalia sat down at the table and continued.

"But he begged me. In a voice so faint that I had to press my ear against his mouth. He said that no granddaughter of his should grow up believing the lies told about music. And that he couldn't die in peace unless he knew you would learn the old ways and sing the old songs."

Zantalalia picked up the teapot and refilled the bowls.

"Now where was I?"

"Grandfather Jessup couldn't die in peace ..." Aurora began.

"Yes. So, of course, I said yes. But I knew there would be trouble. I knew I wouldn't be able to stay for long. So I promised to dig up the Song Spinner and give it to you. The Song Spinner would teach you the songs after I was gone."

Aurora looked longingly at the Song Spinner. She could hardly wait to take it home.

"But that's not possible now," said Zantalalia.

"Why not?"

"It's much too dangerous. Worse than I'd thought. I'd forgotten how zealous the Noise Police could be."

"I'm not afraid," said Aurora.

"I'm sure you're very brave, dear, but I can't expect a young girl to take such a risk."

Aurora ran to the Song Spinner and threw her arms around it. "I could hide it," she said.

"And what if it were found? You'd be in serious trouble. No," said Zantalalia. "I'm afraid it's out of the question."

"But you made a promise to my grandfather."

"That's true," said Zantalalia. She picked up the old wooden box they had just dug up. "But at the time I had no idea. I suppose I had hoped that things might have improved here. But I see the same fearful eyes in the same dull faces. You must help me bury the Song Spinner again."

"Putting it back in the ground won't help to improve things," said Aurora. She picked up the Song Spinner. It was heavy, heavier than it looked. She had never wanted anything more in her life. She would fight to keep it. "You said yourself it belongs to me. I have the right to decide what happens to it. And I have decided that I will take it home and hide it. I know the perfect place where no one will ever find it."

Zantalalia smiled. "I see you've been blessed with your grandfather's stubbornness. Well, I have no more doubts. You *are* Jessup's granddaughter. And the Song Spinner is yours."

Aurora felt as if her heart would sing for joy. She kissed the bird with the turquoise feathers and put the Song Spinner back into the wooden box. Then she found an old sled in the yard and placed the box on the sled. Zantalalia covered it with a red blanket. "One day the Law will be changed," Zantalalia said. "People will want to make music again. But till then, be very careful. It must not fall into the wrong hands."

"I understand," said Aurora.

Zantalalia gave Aurora the magic key and hugged her with a strength that surprised her and made her feel safe.

"In the Water World, we don't say good-bye," said Zantalalia. "We say: *baiya sheetoora*. It means: my music goes with you."

"*Baiya sheetoora*," said Aurora, as she pulled the sled toward the forest. She turned and saw Zantalalia shoveling the dirt back into the hole where the Song Spinner had been sleeping all those years. She was grateful she had helped to wake it up. She would never let it be silenced again.

When she reached the forest, Aurora didn't feel quite so brave. The trees closed in around her, blocking out the sky. It was difficult to see the path. That made it hard to pull the sled, and Aurora worried that her wonderful birthday present might topple over. She pulled the sled gently up and over the roots and stopped several times to straighten the Song Spinner. She gave a sigh of relief when she found the chestnut archway and left the forest behind.

But the danger was not over. From the top of the hill, she saw a Noise Policeman standing below by the river. He held an eyeglass to his face and turned his head slowly. Aurora was sure he had spotted her. She wouldn't go back into the forest, but how could she explain what she was doing here. What if he wanted to inspect the box on her sled?

Then she got an idea. She sat on top of the Song Spinner, spread her cape around it, pointed the sled straight ahead and pushed off with her foot. The sled moved slowly, at first, and then began to pick up speed. At the last moment, she remembered Tibo's string ball, and she managed to scoop it up before the sled really took off, whooshing down the hill.

The Noise Policeman looked up. Aurora smiled a forced tight smile, the kind you make when a distant relative comes to visit. She didn't want him to suspect anything. And what could be more innocent than a child out sledding on a winter afternoon? The Noise Policeman watched her for a moment, and then turned back to his search.

Aurora stopped smiling. She was heading straight for the river. As she held on to the end of the rope, she rolled off the sled and turned it away from the river. The wooden box landed with a thud in the snow. Quickly, Aurora hoisted it back onto the sled. She didn't wait to catch her breath but pulled the sled as fast as she could to put some distance between her and the Noise Policeman.

It was dark when she got home, and as she passed by the pigpen, Pepper greeted her with a warm nose. Aurora thought about her Grandfather Jessup hiding in the pig barn and wondered if he had sung for Pepper, too. Then she realized that Pepper was much too young to have met her grandfather.

There was no time to waste. She must get the Song Spinner safely hidden away. She dragged the sled into the pig barn, a small building with a low ceiling. She found a crate and placed the wooden box inside. She lifted the lid and took one last look at the Song Spinner, *her* Song Spinner. Then she covered it again with the red blanket Zantalalia had given her. She was just about to leave when she heard the barn door open.

Now, Aurora had avoided being swallowed up by the evil jillyjum tree, and she had escaped from the Noise Policeman snooping around the riverbank, but she was caught by the greatest snoop of them all. Her brother, Tibo.

"What you got?" he asked.

"It's nothing. Really," said Aurora.

"Is it a birthday present?" Tibo lifted the blanket to get a look. He stared at the coarse wooden box. "What's inside?"

Aurora pushed his arm away. "Where's Grundle?" she asked. That was the name Tibo had given to his ball of string.

Tibo's eyes widened. He stared at Aurora.

"What's the matter? Cat got your tongue?" And using her whispering voice, she cackled, "Or did it get eaten alive by the jillyjum tree?"

"I knew it. I knew it was you," said Tibo.

Aurora reached into her pocket and handed him the string ball. Tibo rolled it over and over in his hands to make sure none of the strings were missing. When he was certain they weren't, he turned his attention back to the mysterious box.

"Show me it or I'll go tell Mother," he said.

Aurora stood in front of the box and crossed her arms.

Tibo turned and walked to the door. Now what could she do? Tell him the truth? He was too young. He wouldn't understand. And besides, he'd never be able to keep a secret. Tibo opened the door slowly. She couldn't let her mother see the Song Spinner, and she couldn't think where else to hide it.

At the door, Tibo turned to look at her, giving her one last chance. She nodded her head, and Tibo came running back. There was no choice. She'd have to show him the Song Spinner. She'd find a way to make him understand.

"What is it?" asked Tibo, grinning.

"It's something you use to ... play a game," answered Aurora.

"What kind of game?"

"School," replied Aurora, shutting the barn door.

Since Tibo was too young to go to school, this was his favorite game. "All right," he said. "Let's play."

"I'll be the schoolteacher," said Aurora. "And you can be my most clever student."

"Goodie ghostie," said Tibo.

"Boys and girls," said Aurora in her best schoolteacher voice.

Tibo sat on a small stool and held on tightly to Grundle. He loved this.

"You've learned your lessons well. So I have a special treat for you. Today you will hear the truth." She removed the red blanket and took the Song Spinner out of the box. Tibo's eyes grew large with wonder.

Aurora placed the magic key into the top. "May I have a volunteer," she said. Tibo stood up, stuffed Grundle into his pocket and went to stand in front of the class. Aurora asked him to turn the magic key three times to the left. Then she grabbed hold of a golden knob, and the bird with the brightly colored feathers began to spin. When the music started, Tibo was alarmed. He cradled his head in his arms to protect himself.

"It's making noise," said Tibo. "It's making awful noise."

Aurora decided she'd made a terrible mistake. She should never have shown Tibo the Song Spinner. Then she heard Zantalalia's voice: *"Whoever holds the key will speak the truth."* Aurora pulled Tibo's hands from his ears and gave him the magic key. "Listen, Tibo," she said. "Listen as hard as you can."

Soon the music began to enchant him. Tibo saw the key glowing in the dim light. He felt his hand getting warm.

"Isn't it beautiful, Tibo? Isn't it the most beautiful thing in the world?" Tibo's eyes opened wide. His face began to glow. He nodded his head yes.

"It's the goodiest, like a rainbow in my ear."

"But remember, it's just a game. And Mother doesn't want to hear about our silly games."

Tibo nodded his head again.

"Swear on your rabbit's grave?" asked Aurora.

He thought a moment. This was a very serious thing to do. "Yes," he said.

"Good," said Aurora, putting the Song Spinner to rest with Zantalalia's blanket. "But if you ever tell anyone this secret, I promise you your tongue will fallout."

Tibo clamped a hand over his mouth.

CHAPTER SEVEN

"What kept you so long, Aurora?" asked her mother, as she cut a very straight line down the center of the birthday pudding, a dark pudding full of currants and cranberries. "Did you find someone to play with?"

Tibo put his finger to his lips and grinned impishly. Aurora glared at him. "I went for a walk," she told her mother.

"By the river again?"

"No." Aurora hesitated. "Into the forest." She hadn't meant to say that.

"What?"

It was the magic key. She had been holding it inside the pocket of her skirt, and it had made her tell the truth. Quickly, she let go of the key and put her hand on the table.

"You're too young to go there," said Megla.

"I'm old enough now," answered Aurora.

Selmo interrupted. "She is mature for her age, Megla. And children are meant to explore."

"Not in these dangerous times," said Megla, almost raising her voice. "Not when the Noise Police have warned us about a crazy woman ..." Megla didn't finish her sentence. Instead, she took a deep breath and passed a piece of birthday pudding to Aurora.

"Thank you, Mother," said Aurora.

In silence, Megla cut up the rest of the pudding. When everyone had been served, Aurora reached for her fork.

"Aren't you forgetting something?" asked her mother.

What could she have forgotten? Did her mother want to know about the walk in the forest? Then Aurora remembered. It was the Birthday Thanksgiving. Every child in Pindrop was expected to say it before eating the birthday pudding.

"I give thanks to Frilo the Magnificent who gave us the Silent Way. I give thanks to my mother who gave me life. I give thanks to my father who protects me." She paused, and added something new. "And I give thanks to ... Grandfather Jessup...who put the beautiful sounds in my head."

Megla sat down in shock. "Aurora! What's gotten into you?" she said, patting the perfect bun at the back of her head.

Aurora tried to explain. "Well, someone had to put the sounds in my head."

Megla's eyes grew dark. "Where did you hear this? Who's been telling you these lies?"

"And they're not just any sounds. They're ... music. And music makes people happy."

Megla gripped the sides of the table. "Do something, Selmo. Do something about this insolent child."

"Aurora," said her father, sharply. "Not another word. Can't you see you're upsetting your mother?"

"I'm sorry, Mother," said Aurora. And she was sorry. Sorry that she couldn't talk to her parents about Grandfather Jessup. Sorry that they would never understand. It would have to be her secret, hers and Zantalalia's. She picked up a piece of pudding with her fork, and when she bit down, she struck something hard, wrapped inside a piece of silver paper. A shining turquoise stone. "It's beautiful," she said. "Thank you." And when the others went back to eating, she put the stone to her ear to listen for its music.

"It's not fair," said Tibo. "Aurora gets all the presents." Then his face brightened. "But I know a secret."

Aurora kicked Tibo under the table and pointed to her tongue.

"But I promised not to tell anyone," he added quickly.

"Then keep your word," said Selmo, "and finish up. It's time to go to the Whispering Hall."

THE DARK GRAY TOWER of the Whispering Hall stuck straight up into the night sky. Large, black wooden birds with long, pointed beaks kept watch at the side of each door, and stained-glass windows showed the beauty of the earth in all its seasons.

Aurora had never liked the birds. One of her teachers said they had long beaks, so they could pluck out the tongues of children who spoke too loudly. But she loved the windows, especially the one that showed spring with its wispy green trees and blue sky and golden sun. It made her feel warm.

A Noise Policeman stood at attention, guarding the main door. When he saw Aurora's family approaching, he nodded to Selmo and opened the door to let Megla and Tibo inside. Selmo took Aurora by the hand and led her to the side door. Children were seldom allowed in there.

Selmo turned the brass key in the lock. "This way to a special birthday present," he announced as he waved Aurora inside. She followed her father down a long hallway full of marble statues. This was the Hall of Justice—a museum celebrating the victory of silence over noise. Aurora had read about it in history class at school.

She stopped to look at a statue of a lady in a long, white dress. A sash covered both her ears, and she held a finger to her lips as if she were shushing someone who made noise. Next to the silencing lady were two bronze plaques with bold letters. One said *The Vacant Mind Speaks the Loudest*, and the other, *Silence is Golden*.

There was a painting of terrified children, young noise doers, soap bubbles foaming in their mouths, and a large woman leaning over them with a sponge. And another painting of criminals who had lost their tongues to the executioner's sword. And statues, all of them showing what happened to people who made too much noise. Aurora shivered and ran quietly to catch up with her father. He had stopped in front of a large doorway.

Aurora stood behind him and peeked inside. She had never seen such splendor before. A large crystal chandelier was suspended from the ceiling, and mounted on the walls were gleaming silver swords. Aurora thought about the noise doers in the Hall of Justice and clamped her mouth shut. There were dozens of paintings of old men, each with a name underneath it in gold letters. Each and everyone a Frilo—Frilo the Just, Frilo the Fair, Frilo the Jolly.

And then she saw him, Frilo the Magnificent, sitting on a large, gilded throne. She had never seen him up close before. He was an old man. At least, to Aurora he seemed very old, with his long white beard resting like snow on his great pillow of a stomach. He tapped impatiently at a piece of parchment paper with a turkey leg.

"No, no, no, NO!" said Frilo to a servant who was dressed all in white. "We had roasted goose with orange sauce last year. And the year before and the year before that. It's surely time for a change."

Aurora placed her hands lightly over her ears. For the ruler of a peaceful country, he was speaking loudly.

Frilo tore a chunk of meat from the bone and began to chew noisily. "Tell the cook we'll dine on roasted goose with ... with ... oh, I don't care, just make it something different." And he threw the half-eaten bone across the room. With a practiced air, the servant slid across the floor and caught the bone just before it touched the ground. Then he bowed low and walked backwards out of the room, as it was rude to show your back to Frilo the Magnificent.

"And be sure the silver is polished and the pigs' feet are marinated for twenty-four hours," Frilo called out after him. He sat back in his throne and patted his great belly. "No detail can be considered too small. This will be the most glorious Sunwatch celebration in the history of Pindrop."

Frilo dipped a quill pen into an inkwell and scribbled across the parchment. "All these preparations," he said to himself. "Do I really have the stomach for it?"

Aurora giggled nervously. "Shh!" said her father.

Frilo looked up and saw them standing at the door.

"Ah, Selmo. Come in, come in. And this must be your little Aurora." He pressed his fingertips together and peered at her. "Such a nice, quiet girl."

Aurora curtsied uncomfortably. It was all a lie. She wasn't a nice, quiet girl. She didn't want to be a nice, quiet girl. Not anymore. But she didn't dare say a word. Instead, she curtsied again, even more awkwardly, and stared at the floor.

Then something very strange happened. She had the feeling that she was being watched. She looked up at the paintings and saw the Frilos, Just and Fair and Jolly. They narrowed their eyes accusingly at her. Or was it just her imagination? She wanted to run away and hide. Only her mother's careful training kept her from opening her mouth and screaming.

CHAPTER EIGHT

Aurora was relieved when her father took her hand and they left the great room of Frilo the Magnificent. She must have been holding her breath, for suddenly she heard herself take in a quick gulp of air.

"Are you all right?" asked Selmo.

"Yes," said Aurora. "I'm just excited about my birthday present."

They crossed the narrow hallway to reach her father's chamber. As she waited for Selmo to open the door, Aurora noticed another door. A small one with a very large padlock on it, the second one she had seen that day. The first one had locked the door to the old granary where Zantalalia had shown her the beautiful noise makers. Selmo turned to see her looking at the door.

"It leads to an old tower," he said. "No one has been up there for years."

"Why not?" asked Aurora.

"I guess there's no reason to go up there."

"Then why is it locked?"

"Enough questions for one day. Don't you want to see your present?" Of course, she did. And so Aurora forgot about the locked door in the hallway. For now. She followed her father into his private room. It was so small inside that there was just enough space for the two of them. On a tall rack hung his Whispering Robes—white ones, blue ones, a silver one for special occasions. Aurora noticed the sweet smell of mugwort—the same as in her father's study at home. Her father burned it every day. To give him guidance, he said.

Aurora stood between two Whispering Robes while her father took down a large box from a high cupboard. The box was covered in green velvet. She felt a thrill of anticipation as she shut her eyes to make a wish. Nothing could be as magical as the music machine Zantalalia had given her that morning. But she decided to wish anyway—for a new cape to match her red boots.

She opened the box first, then her eyes. Inside was a three-pointed hat, like the Whispering Hat her father wore to give the Tidings. Only smaller. Aurora didn't understand. She forced her lips to make a smile.

Before she could think of something to say, a piercing sound broke the silence. It was Frilo the Magnificent across the hall. Aurora thought something must be terribly wrong. Perhaps the other Frilos were watching *him* now.

"Ooohhh," moaned Frilo. "My aching ears. Why are so many pins dropping in Pindrop? Nizzle! Do something about this infernal noise!" To tell the truth, no one had made a sound as far as Aurora could tell. It was only the snow sliding off the roof.

"Another one of your headaches, Excellency?" Aurora could hear Captain Nizzle's voice saying to Frilo. "Have you forgotten to take your medicine again?"

Aurora shook at the sound of his voice. Then she heard footsteps coming toward her father's room. She turned her back to the door and tried to lose herself among the Whispering Robes.

"Good and peaceful eve to you, Captain Nizzle," she heard her father say. "Do you remember my daughter, Aurora?"

Aurora had no choice. She would have to turn and face the consequences. She placed the Whispering Hat on her head and tugged it down to cover as much of her face as possible. She turned slowly to meet Captain Nizzle, keeping her eyes on the floor. She could feel him examining her when she heard a clap of thunder and, a moment later, the sound of Frilo's voice: "Nizzle!"

Captain Nizzle walked quickly out of the room as Frilo's voice continued to rant. "Why can't you *do* something about this monstrous assault on my eardrums? Why, oh why, did I ever make you Captain of the Noise Police? You told me you could provide the serenity I need to govern this ghastly place. What good is a Hush Law if no one will obey it?"

"That was thunder, Your Excellency," Captain Nizzle's voice said. "The Law doesn't apply to nature."

"Then there's a flaw in the Law," said Frilo. "There must be a flaw. How could that have happened? I won't have it. Think of something, Nizzle."

Captain Nizzle's voice became warm and smooth like the oil in a cooking pot just before it begins to sizzle. "I will need more powers," he said. "My hands are tied until you grant me more power." Then his words became a whisper, and the next thing Aurora heard was her father's voice.

"It suits you to a T," said Selmo, admiring the hat. "Don't you like it?"

"Yes, Father. Thank you." Aurora tried to look grateful.

"Such a long time I waited for you, a child like you, to follow in my footsteps. Your mother and I almost gave up hope. When you were born, it seemed like a miracle. Even the midwife thought so. She held you up for me to see, and she spoke her birth vision: 'This child will find her place in the Whispering Hall,' she said. 'That is her destiny.' And she has never been wrong."

Aurora couldn't understand why the midwife had said that her destiny was in the Whispering Hall. She had never felt at home there. She preferred being outside where she might hear the wind blowing in the trees or the rain splashing on the wooden sidewalks.

Selmo adjusted the hat on Aurora's head. It was too big.

"You'll grow into it," he said. Then he placed Aurora's Whispering Hat back into the velvet box. "It will be here waiting for you. Now go, find your place, and meet me after the Tidings."

Aurora walked quickly down the hallway. She passed Frilo's room and the Hall of Justice, and slipped out the door. She passed the Noise Policeman standing watch at the front door and entered the vestibule at the back of the Whispering Hall.

She was in such a hurry that she almost forgot the Greeting. Inside a small alcove stood a statue of Frilo the Magnificent, a statue so large that when Aurora looked up all she could see was the magnificent belly. She put her hands over her ears, the way her mother had taught her, and bowed to the belly in the statue. Then she lifted the Hush Cloth around her neck to cover her mouth. One had to be especially quiet in the Whispering Hall.

She walked on tiptoe into the great room. A few coal-oil lamps hung from the ceiling, but still the room was gloomy. In the dim light, she saw a sea of faces covered in Hush Cloths, the adults sitting together on the left, the children on the right.

It was torture to walk down the aisle and worry that she might make a squeak on the wooden bench when she sat down. And worst of all was having to sit with the children. She knew they didn't like her. They thought she was strange because of the sounds in her head. No, that midwife had to be wrong for once.

As she entered the children's section, a young girl from her class turned to look at the latecomer. When she saw it was Aurora, she made her large blue eyes cross above her Hush Cloth. The other children sitting next to her did the same.

Aurora felt for the magic key in her pocket. If only they could all hold the key, they would know the truth about the sounds in her head. Then they would understand.

She sat down next to Tibo. He turned and whispered in her ear. "Can I bring my friends home tomorrow to see the music machine?" No! said Aurora with her eyes. Then she looked up at the empty stage and remembered how cheery the Hall had looked in Zantalalia's miniature painting.

When Selmo appeared on the stage, everyone stood up. He wore a pale blue Whispering Robe, the one Aurora liked best. He placed the Whispering Bowl on a stand and spoke over the bowl in a soft whisper that still managed to carry to the back of the Hall. "Welcome all you who gather in silence this evening to pay tribute to our beloved leader, Frilo the Magnificent."

Selmo folded his arms in front of his chest. "May he always shelter us from the noise and discord of a barbarian world. May we all be free to live in golden silence."

Then everyone joined Selmo in the whisper. "We are grateful for the Hush Law that protects us from the dangers of evil noise doers and guarantees all citizens tranquility and peace of mind." Tibo looked up at Aurora. Her mouth was moving, but she wasn't saying the words.

"Today in the silent land of Pindrop, these are the Tidings," said Selmo. He whispered the news of the day, announced the names of those who were having birthdays (Aurora and Pesca the Fisherwoman) and asked for volunteers to help decorate the Whispering Hall.

Then it was time for Captain Nizzle to step forward. He carried a thick, black book with the names of those who had broken the Hush Law. He placed the book down and paused for a moment before beginning in a quiet but serious manner.

"I would like to take this opportunity to stress again the importance of the Hush Cloth. Some of our mothers seem to think it is acceptable to let their babies go about clothless, disturbing the peace with their wailing. Remember, ladies, that infants grow up to be adults. It is never too early to begin proper education in the Silent Way. Vulgar nature may bellow and screech and gaggle and squawk, but humans must rise above such caterwauling. We must not let our precious children become part of this devil's chorus."

He opened his black book and began to read. "Thanks to the valiant efforts of your Noise Police," said Captain Nizzle, "another noise doer, another enemy of the people, has been silenced . . . Lorio the Shopkeeper . . ."

Aurora couldn't believe her ears. Something was very wrong. Lorio wasn't an enemy of the people. He was her friend.

Captain Nizzle continued. " . . . found guilty of breaking the Hush Law for conspiring with evil noise doers."

Evil noise doers! Who did he mean? Aurora wondered.

But she didn't really want to know.

"Lorio will be kept in the Quiet House until after the Sunwatch, at which time he will be transported to the Water World. He will be allowed no visitors."

Aurora bit down hard on her lower lip to stop herself from crying. Even if it had been allowed, she knew no one would have been able to say a word. They didn't dare glance at their neighbors, but hid their frightened faces beneath their Hush Cloths. If Lorio could be arrested, anyone of them might be next.

CHAPTER NINE

After her chores, Aurora ran all the way to Zantalalia's cabin in the forest to tell her what had happened to Lorio at the Whispering Hall the night before.

Now, as she stood at the front door of the cabin, she heard strange noises coming from inside. Not just the noises she'd heard the day before of cupboards closing and floors creaking. These sounds were loud and urgent. POPOPOPOPOPOPOP!

Something terrible was happening to Zantalalia. Aurora pushed against the door and burst into the room. Zantalalia was standing at the wood stove, shaking a pot back and forth. She looked unharmed. But the noise continued. It seemed to be coming from inside the pot. Aurora, her ears covered, watched in amazement as Zantalalia lifted the lid and one white fluffy thing flew out of the pot and landed on the stove, then another.

Zantalalia turned her head, and when she saw the puzzled look on Aurora's face, she smiled. She took a few of the white fluffs and popped them into her mouth. Then she held out the pot to Aurora. Aurora looked inside. She picked one out and put it on her tongue. "It's delicious."

"It's popcorn," said Zantalalia, holding up a jar of unpopped kernels. "It's the heat that makes them explode."

Aurora smiled. Wouldn't her mother be furious if she knew that food could be so noisy? She ate another one and put one into Doremi's birdcage. Then she thought about Lorio again and became serious. She told Zantalalia what little she knew.

"It's all a mistake," Aurora said. "I know it can't be true. Lorio is a good man."

Zantalalia sat down at the kitchen table and sighed. "I'm a tired old woman. And what you've told me has done little to lift my spirits. Poor Lorio. He won't last a week in the Water World."

"Then we must do something to help him."

"I'm afraid I waited too long to return. People have gotten used to all this silence. They don't want some outsider interfering and trying to change things."

"But I do. I'm glad you came back. Now I know about singing and music and the sounds in my head. And I want to learn more. I want to learn all of it."

"What good will that do you?" asked Zantalalia.

"I have a right to know about the old ways. My Grandfather Jessup would want you to show me."

"Show you?"

"Show me how they used to celebrate the Sunwatch in the old days of Shandrilan."

"Well, it's not that simple. We would have to start at the Circle of Stones."

"The Circle of Stones? Is it still here?"

"I suppose so. It was built to last."

"Then show me."

Zantalalia ate a piece of popcorn distractedly. She said nothing.

"Please," said Aurora.

Zantalalia picked up the lamp and reached for her leather pouch.

Aurora grabbed her cape and followed her out the door and into the forest. For an old woman, she walked very quickly. Aurora ran to keep up, until she heard something that frightened her.

It was the sound of wings beating in flight. She looked up and saw a large, black bird, like the one carved out of wood at the entrance to the Whispering Hall.

The bird flew in a graceful circle, turned and headed down toward them. Faster, closer. Aurora covered her head with her arms. She felt the wings brush by her. When the flutter of wings was over, she opened her eyes and saw that the bird was sitting on the old woman's hand. Zantalalia stroked the bird gently as if it were a kitten. Then she lifted her hand, and the bird flew away.

Zantalalia saw the fearful look in Aurora's eyes. "Only those who are afraid of their own freedom will fear the raven. She is the symbol of courage and cunning and freedom."

Soon they left the forest and began walking along the top of the hill. The afternoon sun hovered weakly above the horizon. Zantalalia looked up at the gray sky.

"The days are always short this time of year," she said, "because the sun moves so quickly across the sky."

"I don't like the darkness," said Aurora. "I wish it was always bright and sunny."

"But darkness is also a good thing," said Zantalalia. "It gives plants and animals and people a time to rest. Without darkness, nothing can be born. But, of course, if there is no light, nothing will flower. That's why our great great grandparents began to celebrate the Sunwatch in Shandrilan."

Then she stopped. She stood very still, searching the valley below. Aurora followed her gaze. At first, all she saw were trees and bushes sprinkled with snow. But when she looked in the distance, something quite out of the ordinary appeared. Pillars, tall pillars of white stone that formed a circle. A carved raven spanned huge wings across two of the pillars.

Zantalalia took her hand, and they started down the hill. It was so steep they had to break into a run.

It looked as if no one had set foot inside the circle for years. Bushes covered the narrow path, and snakes of withered ivy climbed up the sides of the stone pillars. Aurora wanted to ask a million questions, but Zantalalia seemed to be in a hurry. She followed the old woman through the bushes.

"Fools," scowled Zantalalia. "They've forgotten how to use the Circle of Stones. How could they possibly know the best time to plant or to harvest?"

"It's amazing!" said Aurora as they walked inside.

"Our ancestors built it thousands of years ago," said Zantalalia. "To follow the path of the sun. On the shortest day of the year, they danced and sang the liveliest songs they knew. To get the sun's attention. To persuade it to slow down and shine its golden lamp upon the earth."

"Can we sing one now?"

Zantalalia looked tired after the long walk, but she agreed.

She opened her pouch and took out a golden shawl. "This shawl belonged to my grandmother and to her grandmother's grandmother." She folded it into a triangle and wrapped it around her shoulders. She took two candles, lit them with the lamp and gave one to Aurora. Then she began to teach Aurora the Sunwatch Hymn, which she had been singing since she was a little girl.

At first, Aurora's voice was unsure. Her father had been training her to whisper. Then a strong wind blew down from the hill and passed through the white pillars. As it swirled around the Circle of Stones, it seemed to stir the voices of the past, the voices of Jessup and all the others who had been here before her. Now the singing came out easy, and the chorus rang out strong and true:

Keeper of the sky garden
Torch of the gods
Warm our land
Our Shandrilan.

Zantalalia's eyes brightened. "What a lovely voice," she said. "Sweet and clear. What did I tell you? You do have Jessup's talent. Your song would be sure to get the sun's attention." And then she frowned. "But tomorrow at the Sunwatch, there will be no music."

"Well, even if the Sunwatch is silent," said Aurora, "the sun comes back to us anyway."

"But does it? Do you see much sunshine in the faces of

your family? Your neighbors?"

Aurora thought about the faces of people she knew: the stern face of her mother, the mean face of Unso the Milkman and the cross-eyed faces in the Whispering Hall. Zantalalia was right.

"All you see is fear and darkness. Who knows? If we have another silent Sunwatch, the sun may disappear forever."

Zantalalia looked deep into Aurora's eyes. "There is a terrible darkness here in Pindrop. The worst kind. A darkness of the heart. But music is your candle glowing in that darkness. Remember what I have taught you, Aurora. And never let your flame go out."

"I promise," said Aurora, and she began to follow Zantalalia back up the hill. It was getting dark now, but she wished she could stay in the Circle of Stones. She felt she belonged there with the memory of those ancient people who must also have heard sounds in their heads.

Then she remembered a not-so-ancient person who was in a lot of trouble. "What about Lorio?"

Zantalalia stopped and announced, "I've made up my mind. I'm going to Frilo."

"What?" said Aurora. She could hardly believe her ears.

"I'll see him tomorrow morning and talk some sense into him."

"But he won't speak to you. He thinks you're an evil noise doer."

"He didn't always think that."

"You know him?"

"Shush, child. Didn't anyone ever teach you that silence is golden?" Zantalalia smiled a mysterious smile.

The whole idea made Aurora very nervous. Going to Frilo seemed an impossibly dangerous thing to do. "What if the Noise Police stop you before you can speak to him?"

Zantalalia paused to consider.

"I'll write a letter." She took a piece of paper and a stick of charcoal from her pouch. She sat on the ground against a tree and wrote quickly. When she finished, she handed Aurora a letter addressed to Frilo the Magnificent. "If I don't come back, you must deliver this letter to Frilo."

Aurora was frightened. She couldn't imagine losing Zantalalia. She threw her arms around the old woman. *"Baiya sheetoora,* my dear, Aurora," said Zantalalia, and she held her close.

They heard a loud, snapping noise, like a twig cracking. A Noise Policeman was patrolling the edge of the forest. Zantalalia pulled Aurora down and waited until he had moved on. "Go now," she whispered. And Aurora ran with the wind along the side of the hill.

With the moon following her along the riverbank, she clutched the letter that could save her people from darkness. Suddenly, she heard a loud voice. "Halt! Who's there?"

Aurora stopped. In the moonlight, she saw the silhouette of a Noise Policeman coming toward her. She grasped the letter more tightly and began to run.

"I order you to stop," said the voice again.

But Aurora continued to push into the darkness, the wind swirling about her, whipping her hair in all directions. She didn't notice the large rock in her path. Her boot caught the edge of it and down she fell, dropping the precious letter.

Before she could scramble up to fetch it, a gust of wind snatched it and carried it off. It whirled on the ground like a spinning top, then swayed back and forth until finally it lifted high into the air. The Noise Policeman danced about underneath it, his hands darting out to grab for it, but it sailed even higher. While the Noise Policeman chased after the letter, Aurora ran in the opposite direction. When she was far enough away, she stopped and turned. The wind had changed direction, and the letter stopped in mid-flight. It dropped straight down, fluttered over the rocks, landed on the water and the River of Sorrow carried it away.

CHAPTER TEN

Aurora cried all the way home. Her eyes were red, and her stomach felt like a hollow ball. She hung up her cape and took the magic key out of her pocket, but it only made her feel worse. Then, quite unaware that she was doing it, she started to hum a sad tune.

"Aurora?" It was her mother's voice. "Is that you?" Aurora stopped humming. She hid the magic key behind her back. There in the kitchen doorway were her mother and father frowning at her.

"Where did you learn to do that?" Selmo demanded. Aurora decided she would have to tell a lie to protect Zantalalia. Maybe she could blame it on one of the children at school, or she could pretend that she hadn't done anything. That sometimes worked with parents. But before she could lie, she heard herself saying, "I learned it from the music machine."

Aurora watched as her mother's mouth formed a silent scream, and her father's face grew pale. She had no other choice now. She would have to take her parents to the pig barn and show them Zantalalia's birthday present.

ALL THREE WERE SILENT in the barn as Aurora lifted the red blanket.

"A noise machine!" said Selmo at last, bending his head under the low ceiling.

"A Song Spinner," said Aurora.

"This is blasphemy," said her mother.

"No," said Aurora, not understanding the word. "It's the most beautiful present I ever got."

She hadn't meant to tell them that.

"Listen to her, Selmo," said Megla. "Listen to your daughter. The one you spoiled all these years. See how she repays you."

"How could you do this to me?" asked Selmo. And the disappointment in his voice made Aurora feel even emptier.

Megla took Aurora by the shoulders. "Don't you understand? The Hush Law forbids it. It's the Quiet House for all of us if anyone finds out."

Aurora didn't think her parents would listen, but she tried to explain anyway. "Mother, Father, the Song Spinner could save us."

Megla scowled. Selmo tried to control himself. "Where did you get it?" he asked.

"You were with that crazy woman, weren't you?" said Megla.

"She's not crazy," said Aurora. "She's just ... unusual. And she makes the most beautiful music. Listen." Aurora placed the magic key into the Song Spinner. But Megla stopped her. "The only thing I want to hear is the sound of this contraption being chopped into bits."

"We'd never get a noise permit," said Selmo, trying to be reasonable.

"Let the Noise Police take care of it," said Megla.

"Out of the question. Then we'd have to explain where we got it."

"Bury it in the forest, then," Megla suggested.

"No, no!" cried Aurora.

"I won't have this thing here," said Megla. "I won't. I won't."

"Be quiet," said Selmo. "Both of you. Tomorrow morning, I'll take it from here and throw it into the river. That's final."

He picked up the Song Spinner and placed it into the wooden box.

"Not till tomorrow?" asked Megla. "I'll never be able to sleep knowing it's here."

"It's too dark to move it somewhere else," answered Selmo. "And here, at least, it's well hidden."

He covered the box with the red blanket and looked sternly at Aurora. "And you're never to have anything more to do with this machine."

That night, Aurora slept fitfully. She dreamed she was swimming in the river, and no matter how hard she swam, the Song Spinner bobbed along in the water a few feet from her grasp. She woke up just as it was about to crash into a large rock. She got out of bed and went to the window.

She looked out at the pig barn and thought about the Song Spinner and all the songs she had yet to learn. She tiptoed out of her bedroom and ran to the barn.

She picked up the red blanket and put it around her shoulders. It was an ordinary wool blanket with holes where the moths had been. But it had belonged to Zantalalia and so it kept her warm.

Aurora put the magic key into the Song Spinner and played the first song over and over again. When she knew it well enough, she began to sing along very quietly. She learned other songs, songs about planting corn and raising children, songs about courage and love. Once or twice, she thought she heard a noise outside. She decided it was just the wind. When she was exhausted, she put her head in her hands and began to weep. Suddenly, the door opened. It was her father.

"How can you continue to disobey me?" he asked in a tired, sad voice.

"It's so beautiful, Father. How can anyone say it's bad?" she said through her tears.

"It's against the Hush Law," answered Selmo.

"Then it's the Law that's bad."

"Children are not the judge of these things," Selmo said.

But he moved, as if pulled by a string, toward the Song Spinner. His hand, as if it didn't belong to him, took hold of a golden knob and turned it. And as the beautiful bird flew round and round, the Song Spinner played a song that made him listen with his heart. Aurora wondered if he had heard this song before. Perhaps when he was a very young child, before the Hush Law.

When the music was over, Selmo sat down beside Aurora and put his arm around her.

"Please don't throw the Song Spinner into the river," Aurora begged.

Selmo looked into Aurora's pleading face and made a quick decision. "I'll take it back to the old woman. Early in the morning, I'll take it and leave it on her doorstep. But you must promise never to see her again." Then he reached for another golden knob, but something made him stop. He held his hand in midair for a moment, and then it fell to his lap.

It didn't matter what her father believed. Aurora was happy that she had learned the old songs. When the Law was changed, she would be ready.

EARLY THE NEXT MORNING, Aurora watched sadly as her father placed the Song Spinner onto the sled and secured it in place with a long piece of thick twine.

Her mother came out of the house with two gray wool blankets. "I think you've lost your mind, Selmo. But I won't let you go alone." She wrapped one blanket around Selmo's shoulders and pulled it up over his head so no one would recognize him. She put the other blanket over herself.

"I'll come with you," said Aurora. "You might have trouble finding the cabin." But Aurora had already traced the directions in the snow for her father.

"Go in the house and get to your whispering," said Selmo as he pulled the sled away.

With a heavy heart, Aurora watched them go. Pepper came by, sniffing at some dried grasses poking out of the snow. She patted his head and went into the house.

Inside her father's study, Aurora picked up the Whispering Bowl. She took a deep breath, but nothing happened. She tried again. After all Zantalalia had taught her, she couldn't make herself whisper. She dropped the bowl and began to sing. *Fortissimo.* The house seemed to shake with the unusual sound.

Tibo entered from his bedroom. He was still in his nightshirt, and he carried his string ball. "On the single, on the double, noisy people get in trouble," he whispered. Aurora wanted to tell him to be quiet when she realized that being quiet was part of the problem.

"Louder," she said. "Say it louder, Tibo. I can't hear you." Tibo recited the rhyme again, a little louder this time.

"I still can't hear you," said Aurora as she rushed by Tibo.

She paused long enough to grab her cape and continued running out the door. Tibo followed her.

"On the single," he started. When he realized he was shouting, he put his hand over his mouth and went straight back into the house.

Aurora didn't stop running until she caught sight of the sled and the two gray blankets. She followed them along the river, up the hill and into the forest, hanging back so they couldn't see her.

When the gray blankets reached Zantalalia's cabin, Aurora hid behind a tree and watched. The door opened and there stood Zantalalia, her hair uncombed, her eyes fierce. She looked like a witch in a fairy tale.

"You must be Aurora's parents," she heard Zantalalia say. "Come in quickly. You're in danger outside."

She saw her mother step back. But her father took her by the hand and pulled her into the cabin after him.

Aurora ran quickly across the clearing and around the side of the cabin to look through a window. She found one that was low enough and clean enough to peer through. Her father had placed the Song Spinner on the kitchen table. Her mother was standing by the table, dusting the edge of it with her blanket. Her lips were moving, but Aurora couldn't hear what she was saying. Nor could she hear her father. Only Zantalalia's voice was loud enough to carry through the window.

"Do you think it natural to be always silent?" asked Zantalalia. "Does the wind not howl in the trees? Does the ocean not break against the rocks?"

Aurora saw her mother scowl. She could imagine what Megla was saying: that humans should know better than to imitate the vulgar noises of nature, and that the Silent Way was the only way.

"Of course, silence can be a wonderful thing," said Zantalalia. "It allows you to hear the special music inside you. Why, you listen and listen, and after a while, the sound just pours out of you like clear spring water."

Megla raised her voice. "Rubbish. All rubbish. You ... you old witch, you should be ashamed of yourself, filling Aurora's head with this ... this fanciful talk, giving her a noise machine and putting her life in danger."

"Aurora's life was in danger before I arrived," said Zantalalia. "Do you really want her to live in the dark the way you have?"

Her mother didn't want to hear another word. She grabbed Selmo's arm. "It's time to go, Selmo. We must think of Aurora's future."

"Aurora will have no future worth living if you don't help her," replied Zantalalia.

Aurora saw her father move closer to Zantalalia, and she listened with a heavy heart to her father's frightened voice. "Aurora has a future with me, with her mother. A great future in the Whispering Hall."

Zantalalia smiled sadly at him. "Aurora will never be a whisperer. She was born to sing. To make music like her grandfather. If you try to stop her, you will lose her forever."

When Aurora saw her father's face, so shaken, so pale, she wanted to weep. He had been so good to her, had loved her so much. And now he knew the truth. She could never be what he wanted her to be.

Zantalalia reached into her pocket and removed a small piece of rice paper. It was the painting she had shown Aurora on her birthday. She held it up for them to see.

Megla turned her head away. But Selmo looked at it very carefully. Then Zantalalia started up the Song Spinner, and soon the old cabin hummed with music. Music that made you feel like moving your body back and forth.

Megla screwed up her face and covered her ears while Selmo stared into the painting. Aurora could not hear his soft, sad words, but it was clear that the painting had stirred in him some long-ago memory of Shandrilan, before the beautiful sounds had been outlawed.

Out of the corner of her eye, Megla caught a glimpse of the painting. She reached out quickly, snatched it from Selmo, and with a sharp twist, ripped it in half.

Not the beautiful painting! Aurora banged her fist against the window and shouted, "How could you? How could you?"

She stopped shouting when she saw that her mother was crying. She had never seen her cry before. Not a single tear. She was surprised at the way her mother's hands were shaking and how she pulled at her hair, making a mess of the perfect bun at the back of her head. Aurora wanted to run in and hold her and comfort her. But as she pulled away from the window, she saw something moving in the forest. In fact, the whole forest seemed to be moving.

It was the Noise Police. And at the head was Captain Nizzle in his black chariot. The chariot swayed perilously over the rough ground until it came to a sudden stop at a large root. Four Noise Policemen rushed over and lifted the chariot over the root. Captain Nizzle bounced along the path again, clutching the reins.

Aurora stumbled toward the cabin door. How could the Noise Police have found the cabin? she wondered. Had they followed her? Had they forced Lorio to tell?

At last she got to the front door. She flew into the room and into Zantalalia's arms.

"The Noise Police," she said, out of breath, "the Noise Police are coming!"

CHAPTER ELEVEN

"**G**o down to the cellar," said Zantalalia. "And hurry." She threw open the cellar door, and Aurora started down the ladder. Megla followed behind her. The ladder was steep and she went down slowly, shaking with fear.

"Come with us," said Selmo.

"No," said Zantalalia. "I will stay with the Song Spinner."

"But they'll arrest you."

"That may be the only way," said Zantalalia, as she motioned Selmo to the ladder. "If it's not safe to come out, take the tunnel. It leads to the edge of the clearing." She pulled another knob on the Song Spinner and smiled as the music filled the room.

When they were all inside the cellar, Zantalalia closed the door over them. Aurora felt her father's arm around her shoulder. They waited in the darkness. Then Aurora heard Zantalalia's voice cry out, "The blankets!" The gray blankets that her mother and father had worn as a disguise had been left upstairs. At the same moment, a pair of strange boots crossed the threshold and stomped above them.

"Silence that wretched thing," said an angry voice. It was Captain Nizzle.

The Song Spinner was silenced. More boots arrived. To Aurora below, it sounded like thunder as the boots crashed against the wooden floor, kicking and prodding and probing. She could hear cupboards being opened and things being tossed about.

"Arrest that woman for not wearing a Hush Cloth," said Captain Nizzle. "And for disturbing the peace with an illegal noise machine and on suspicion of treason."

"Yes, Captain," said a voice.

"Bind her hands, and help her on with this Hush Cloth." Aurora winced. She knew it would be a very scratchy one.

"And there were two others," Captain Nizzle said. "Wearing gray blankets."

"I'm sure I don't know what you mean," said Zantalalia.

"You'll tell me the truth, woman."

Then Aurora heard Sergeant Goth's voice. "There are two gray blankets over here on the bed, Captain."

Zantalalia laughed through her Hush Cloth. "Why, they've been in the family for years. And besides, they're as common as lice. I'm sure you have some at home yourself."

"Any more bright ideas, Goth?" asked Captain Nizzle.

"If it's high quality blankets you're looking for," said Zantalalia, "the best place to find them is at Lorio's store, unless, of course, you've had to close it down because of the Hush Law."

"Hogwash," said Captain Nizzle. "I have more important things to do than to engage in idle chitchat with a demented old busybody."

Then a pair of light, quick boots rushed in. "There's no one outside, Captain."

"Incompetents!" growled Captain Nizzle. "Get the bloodhounds, Constable Callo. They'll do a better job of it. Look alive, Callo. Goth, take the Water World woman. Step to it. I want no more foul-ups. No mistakes."

All of a sudden the storm was over. The boots were gone.

Aurora thought she could hear Zantalalia singing through her Hush Cloth.

The door closed, and after a few moments of silence, she ran up the ladder. "Wait," said her father. But she opened the cellar door a crack. "They're all gone," she said.

She crawled out and looked around the room in horror.

It was as if someone had put all the contents into a large bag, shaken them up and dumped them out again. Zantalalia was gone and so was the birdcage. Under the kitchen table, she found half of the rice paper painting, and across the room, the other half face down on the floor, the outline of a boot on its back. She stuffed the two halves into her pocket—she would find a way to put them back together later—and dashed to the window. She saw Sergeant Goth carrying the Song Spinner on his shoulder like a trophy. Inside the black chariot stood Zantalalia, her hands tied behind her back. Next to her was Captain Nizzle. He wrote something in his black book and stuffed it in his pouch. "Onward, Whist!" he commanded.

Aurora was surprised at what happened next. Captain Nizzle's horse didn't budge. Instead, he shook his head from side to side as if he were being bothered by a bumble bee or a mosquito. Captain Nizzle scowled. "On the double, Whist!" Again, Whist shook his head. Captain Nizzle leaped out of the chariot to see what was the matter. At once, Whist became very still, then turned to look at Zantalalia, nodded twice and began to pull the chariot forward. Captain Nizzle ran after them, waving his fists in the air. At last he caught up to them and threw himself into the rig. He held tight to the reins and frowned menacingly at Zantalalia.

As Aurora watched them go, she heard footsteps on the floor behind her.

"Get back to the cellar," her father whispered as he took her position at the window.

Frightened, she ran down the cellar ladder in two steps. In the dim light she saw her mother sitting on a wooden crate. When she got closer, she noticed that her eyes were still red from crying. "I knew it. I knew it," her mother was saying. "I knew this would happen."

Aurora took her mother's hand and squeezed it. There were so many things she wanted to know. Why her mother had cried. Why she had torn up the magic painting. But she was afraid to say anything, and she felt sure her mother would blame her for all of this.

After a while, her mother spoke. "When I was your age, Aurora, I had a father who loved to make noise."

"The one who plays the horn in the painting," said Aurora quietly.

"Yes. That was your Grandfather Jessup. A wonderful man. But stubborn. The Noise Police took him away with the others in the middle of the night. I woke up one morning, and he was gone. I never saw him again."

Aurora waited for her mother to continue.

"It wasn't easy to grow up without a father. And to have to bear the shame of his crimes against the Hush Law. When you started talking about the sounds, those sounds in your head...don't you understand? All I ever wanted was for you to be quiet. So I wouldn't lose you, too."

"He came back," said Aurora.

Megla frowned.

"It's true. He came back when I was a baby, and that's when he put the sounds in my head."

Suddenly, Megla smiled—was it the first time Aurora had seen her smile? And she looked at her in a way Aurora had never seen before. As if the two of them had shared a wonderful secret. Then her mother took the ivory pins from her hair, and the perfect bun disappeared. Aurora saw something fall out of her mother's hair. It was a thin, gold chain with a heart-shaped locket. She gave it to Aurora. Aurora held it gently in her hand and opened the lid. Inside was a miniature painting of a man playing a long brass horn.

"He would want you to have it," said her mother. "But you mustn't show it to your father."

Aurora heard footsteps coming down the ladder and was relieved to see it was her father. He shut the door behind him, and in the dark, his voice sounded ominous. "The Noise Police are watching the cabin. We'll have to use the tunnel."

The tunnel wasn't easy to find in the dark. They moved cautiously among the boxes and barrels until they came to a place where the room narrowed.

Aurora held onto her father with one hand and used the other to feel along the edge of the wall. Earth. Cool and moist. She heard her mother on the other side, groping along the narrow tunnel. They had walked a few minutes like this when suddenly the wall became bumpy. Tree roots! They must be at the edge of the clearing. They could go no further underground.

Aurora's father hoisted her onto his shoulders, and she moved her hands across the ceiling. "It feels like wood," said Aurora.

"Push," said her father. And when she did, the wooden plank lifted. Aurora's eyes, which had gotten used to the dark tunnel, closed for a moment against the light. In the distance, she could see the Noise Policemen patrolling the cabin. Her father gave her a shove, and she landed on a soft carpet of snow and moss. Aurora put her hand back into the tunnel to help her mother out and then her father. They were all outside the tunnel when they heard a rustling in the bushes. It was the bloodhound.

Aurora and her parents began to make their way through the forest. They moved as fast as they could, but the dog came nearer. They would never be able to outrun it. When they stopped behind a bush to rest, they heard the animal panting. "It's no use," whispered Aurora's mother.

At that moment they saw the dog sniffing the ground. He was followed by Constable Callo. As if that wasn't bad enough, another animal was scurrying through the bushes. A small, furry black creature with a white stripe down its back. Aurora closed her eyes and held her breath. She thought of Zantalalia. She imagined the old woman speaking gently to the skunk, reassuring him they meant no harm. When she opened her eyes, the skunk had changed directions and was heading straight for Constable Callo.

The hound became very agitated at the sight of the skunk. He tugged at the leash. He was ready for sport. Constable Callo saw the skunk, too, and he pulled back hard on the leash. The tug-a-war continued. Back and forth. Back and forth until at last the dog won. The leash snapped, and he leaped toward the skunk. Suddenly he stopped, stood his ground and took a deep sniff. Then he turned and bounded in the direction of Callo, who was running away from him at top speed.

Chapter Twelve

"Dear Frilo the Magnificent," Aurora wrote in her neatest handwriting.

Her worst fear had come true. Zantalalia had been arrested. And since she had lost the letter Zantalalia had given her, she would have to write her own and tell Frilo all the things her new friend had explained to her.

When she had finished, she sealed the envelope with pink wax and left the house before the others woke up. Before anyone could stop her. Ever since yesterday's adventure in the forest, her mother had become even more anxious. She would never let Aurora go out by herself.

The morning was cool and dark. No one was around to see her. She tucked the letter inside her cape and ran along the empty streets. She put a hand into her pocket and felt her father's brass key, the one that opened the side door of the Whispering Hall. Before leaving the house, she had gone into his study and found it on the hook by the door where he always kept it. She would have to return it before her father noticed it was missing.

At the side door of the Whispering Hall, she hid behind the wings of the wooden raven. She remembered that Zantalalia had told her this was the bird of courage and freedom, and she felt less afraid. She waited until the guard walked by. Then she turned the key in the lock, opened the door and went inside. She tiptoed down the grand hallway, into the Hall of Justice, past the statue of the lady in the long white dress telling everyone to be quiet. Past the paintings of those who had lost their tongues.

She stopped at Frilo's door and slipped the letter underneath. She turned to go back the same way she had come when she heard someone walking toward her. She would have to keep going. Perhaps she could go into her father's chamber and hide behind the Whispering Robes.

But before she could enter, she heard a noise coming from her father's room. She was sure he was at home in bed. Who could it be? She moved swiftly and quietly down the hallway.

She came to the door leading to the old tower. But now the padlock was gone. The footsteps in the hall were coming nearer. She opened the door and slipped inside, closed the door and pressed her back against it.

Straight up from the door were steep, narrow stairs, and at the very top, a faint light. The tiny steps were just big enough for her feet.

The stairs opened into a large room, with windows all around letting in the first frail light of morning. The room was full of books, even more than in her father's study at home. They were yellow and dusty and smelled like wet leaves in the fall. She picked one up and blew the dust from it. It was called *The History of Shandrilan*. Another was called *The Singing Birds of Shandrilan*. And another, *The Art of Music*.

Aurora gasped. Here were stories she longed to read. Stories about the musical days in Shandrilan and about those who knew how to sing. How could anyone have hidden them away? She felt so angry she wanted to stamp her feet. Instead, she thought of how she might take a few of the books with her when she left.

A flash of light from near the window caught her attention. It was a long brass tube. Another music maker? Aurora wondered. She touched the cool brass. There were no valves to make it play and no bell for the sound to come out. She looked into the narrow end. This was amazing. She could see the forest as if it were right there in the room. The trees were so close, she felt she could almost touch them. This was much better than Lorio's eyeglasses, which made things only a tiny bit bigger.

She leaned against the brass tube and it moved. She looked inside again, and when she focused her eye, she saw Zantalalia's cabin. Someone had been watching them!

Aurora heard a gurgling sound—like water flowing from a well. She turned quickly toward the sound. She saw a red velvet armchair, and hanging over the edge of the chair was a large hand with fat fingers like five pink sausages. It was Frilo the Magnificent. He was snoring.

Aurora's heart sank. How could Zantalalia have been so wrong? This Frilo the Magnificent would never help them. He wouldn't listen. He had been spying on them. He must be the one who had Zantalalia arrested. She wished she had never delivered the letter. And now she had to get out of this room before he discovered her.

But there was a noise on the stairs. She ducked behind a stack of books and waited. The stairs groaned under the weight of heavy boots. Aurora heard a thump and a cough. The snoring stopped.

"Oh, my dear. Oh, my goodness," sputtered Frilo the Magnificent. "Oh, it's you, Nizzle."

Aurora shivered at the sound of that name. But she dared to peek through a gap in the books.

"What is it now?" asked Frilo, and the five pink sausages began to stroke the snowy white beard. "You haven't come to tell me about that Water World woman again, have you?"

"Your Excellency," said Captain Nizzle. Aurora held her breath and listened.

"From the moment she was placed in the Quiet House, she has created one disturbance after another."

"Disturbance? What kind of disturbance?"

"She howls. She sings. She barks. And it's useless to gag her. She hums so loudly and at such a high pitch it could split your ear in two."

He held up something that Aurora recognized immediately. It was Zantalalia's necklace—a circle of delicate, pearly seashells. "I removed this noisy little trifle from her neck."

Frilo took the necklace and gazed at it for a long time before he spoke. "Has she asked to see me?" And Aurora thought his voice sounded like Tibo's when he wanted something very badly but didn't want you to know it.

"She's crazy," said Captain Nizzle. "A lunatic. Going on about the darkness and trying to get the sun's attention. She must be stopped. Of course, I wouldn't dream of letting her see you. It would be unseemly for you to be subjected to her shenanigans. In fact, I've drawn up the papers to have her returned to the Water World immediately."

"Well, yes. I suppose," said Frilo. "On the other hand ... oh, I don't know. It's all too much of a muchness."

Aurora heard the stairs groaning again. She saw a servant carrying a tray of food—fresh fruit, boiled eggs, and ham and biscuits, the kind of breakfast her mother served only once a year, on the morning after the Sunwatch. In spite of her fear, Aurora felt her mouth begin to water. She had left home without breakfast so as not to wake anyone.

Aurora saw Frilo dismiss the servant with a wave of his hand. Her stomach ached as she watched the wonderful food turn away. Just as it was about to disappear down the stairs, Captain Nizzle plucked a ripe peach from the fruit bowl and began to suck the juices from it very gently.

Frilo was speaking again. But this time he sounded more like Aurora's mother when she had made up her mind about something.

"Bring her here," he said to Captain Nizzle. "There's a cell in the basement."

"That cell hasn't been used in years."

"The walls are thick," said Frilo. "She'll find it hard to disturb anyone there."

"Yes. Yes," said Captain Nizzle. "Excellent plan, Excellency. Excellent."

Captain Nizzle wiped his mouth and hands very delicately with a silk cloth. He walked to a wicker basket and dropped the peach pit inside. As he turned, his cape swirled over the dusty books. Aurora held her nose between two fingers and breathed through her mouth to make sure she wouldn't sneeze this time.

"We must show these noise doers we mean business," said Captain Nizzle. "I've done what I can under the limited powers you've given me. My men are working day and night to protect you. But all these precautions are of little value unless you trust me completely to deal with this conspiracy. You have more important things to concern yourself with ...the color of the new drapes for the Whispering Hall, next week's menu."

"Yes, that's true," said Frilo. "All very important things. But do you really believe it? I mean a conspiracy?"

"Yes," said Captain Nizzle. "An underground movement with only one purpose. To overthrow your government and unseat you from your royal throne."

Frilo the Magnificent clutched the arms of his chair.

"How could that be? I thought my people liked me. They need me. I'm the one keeping them safe from noise and chaos. Oh, it's just the time of year, my goodness, and all this darkness. It makes everyone so restless."

"And all this Sunwatch business," said Captain Nizzle. "It only makes matters worse. Stirring up memories that are best forgotten. You should have abolished it years ago." And under his breath he added, "Superstitious malarkey."

"It's a noble tradition," said Frilo. "Celebrated through generations and generations of Frilos."

"Then let's have an old-fashioned celebration," said Captain Nizzle, his voice sounding strange. "I'll order my men to take the music machine and the other noise makers and pile them up in the Great Square. And tonight, during the Sunwatch, I'll set a torch to them all. I've been wanting to do that for years. That should light up the sky. That should get the sun's attention."

"Oh, my heavens," said Frilo. "I suppose it's for the best." He lifted the seashell necklace, and it shook in his hands, making a sound that reminded Aurora of a gentle breeze.

"Of course, it's for the best," said Captain Nizzle, glaring at the seashell necklace. "But now I must take care of that Water World woman." And the next thing he did gave Aurora such a fright that she pinched her lips together to stop from crying out. Captain Nizzle opened his black book, the one with the names of those who had broken the Hush Law. He took the necklace from Frilo, placed it between two pages and snapped the book shut. From her hiding place, Aurora could hear the tiny, delicate shells shattering like glass. Then Captain Nizzle started down the stairs.

Aurora felt tears falling onto her cheeks. Stop it, she thought. There's no time for that. You've got to find a way out of here. Then she heard a small sniffing sound.

She looked up and saw that Frilo was also crying.

Aurora's mind was in a muddle. There was no one to help her now. Not Frilo. Not Zantalalia. She would have to get herself out of this place. And as soon as possible. She waited until the stairs were silent, and waited again until Frilo began to snore. She got up slowly from behind the books, her muscles stiff from crouching. She placed one foot lightly on the top stair. And another . . .

From the bottom of the stairs, she heard Frilo mutter, "You've gone too far, Nizzle. It's all gone too far."

She opened the door and looked out. No one was there. She went quickly and silently down the hall and out the side door.

CHAPTER THIRTEEN

After supper, Aurora and Tibo were sent for a short nap before it was time to go to the Sunwatch.

Aurora tossed in her bed. Nothing could make her feel happy, not Zantalalia's red blanket on her bed, not the rice paper painting, which she had sewn together with the tiniest, neatest stitches.

Tibo sat up in bed and played with Grundle, tossing it into the air and catching it. "We're going to the Sunwatch. We're going to the Sunwatch," he said over and over.

"I'm not going," said Aurora.

Tibo caught the ball and stared at her. "Not going? Not going to the Sunwatch? You'll miss all your presents."

"Presents are for children," said Aurora.

"Can I have yours then?" asked Tibo.

"Good night, Tibo," Aurora snapped.

"Good night," said Tibo, stuffing the string ball under his pillow.

He sounded so hurt that Aurora felt sorry she had spoken so coldly.

"In the Water World, they don't say good night," she said more gently. "They say *baiya sheetoora*. It means, My music goes with you."

Tibo looked at her, puzzled.

"As if you would go to sleep with a beautiful noise in your ear," she said, trying to explain.

Tibo stuck one finger into his ear. "Nothing there," he said.

Aurora turned onto her back and stared at the ceiling.

What did it matter? The Sunwatch would be silent. The Song Spinner was locked away. And so was Zantalalia. Captain Nizzle was going to burn all the noise makers. There would be no music, and the darkness would continue. It was better to stay home.

Then Aurora heard Zantalalia's voice saying, "*Music is your candle glowing in the darkness.*"

Aurora got out of bed quickly. She reached into a dresser drawer and took out a candle. She went to the closet, got a canvas sack and put the candle inside, adding matches and a small knife. Tibo watched her from his bed.

"What are you doing?" he asked.

"Just getting ready for the Sunwatch."

"Are you playing a game?"

"No, Tibo. No more games."

"But I want to play a game."

Aurora looked up at Tibo. He was sitting on the bed, dangling his feet over the edge.

"I know!" said Aurora. "I'll find you a Sunwatch cookie before we leave for the Whispering Hall, and you can play Eat the Cookie."

Tibo decided this would be a fine game to play. "Goodie ghostie," he said and lay down for his nap.

Aurora wrapped the red blanket around her shoulders. It was time to make a plan.

A LIGHT SNOW was falling as Aurora and Tibo followed their parents through the crisp winter night. Aurora pushed a doll carriage that her father had mounted on skis. It whisked gently over the snow.

"Why'd you bring your stupid doll?" asked Tibo. "You never play with her anymore."

"Shh," said Aurora.

She handed Tibo a Sunwatch cookie—a circle of dough with a rising sun in pink icing.

When they got near the Whispering Hall, they saw Noise Policemen working in the Great Square. They were stacking musical instruments onto a huge pile. The night echoed with the tinkling sound of brass on brass, and strings accidentally plucked. Torches, attached to poles in the ground, formed an eerie semicircle around the instruments.

Captain Nizzle prodded his men. "Faster. Faster. I want them all to roast tonight."

Suddenly, Aurora saw Constable Callo place the long horn onto the pile. She grabbed her mother's arm. "Stop him!" cried Aurora. "That was Grandfather Jessup's."

"Hush," said her mother.

"Oh, Father," said Aurora. "You can't let them do it."

"Don't look, Aurora," said Selmo. He came around behind her and helped her push the carriage to the Whispering Hall.

"Jessups? Who is Jessups?" Tibo wanted to know.

Inside the Whispering Hall, pine boughs and holly decorated the walls, but the place was still dark and dreary. Not at all like the Hall in the rice paper painting, thought Aurora.

She sat, holding her doll, beside Tibo in the children's section. Everyone wore Hush Cloths over their mouths. There was even a tiny one for Aurora's doll. The Sunwatch dancers moved slowly down the center aisle, all of them wearing long, black robes, except for the young girl in the center who represented the sun. She was dressed in pale yellow. They danced deliberately, silently, on the tips of their toes. They were graceful, but it seemed to Aurora that the dance had no meaning, or that its meaning had been long forgotten.

Aurora tapped Tibo on the knee. "I've got to do something," she whispered in his ear. "Stay here."

Aurora slipped from her seat and walked up the side aisle to the back of the Whispering Hall. She checked to see if her mother had noticed, but everyone was busy watching the dancers. As soon as she got outside, a Noise Policeman stopped her.

She stood on tiptoe to whisper in his ear that she must see her father, Selmo the Whisperer, before the Tidings. He nodded, and she went around the side of the building. Through the falling snow, she saw a flicker of torches in the distance. She would never let them burn the Song Spinner. She reached the doll carriage, took out the canvas sack and walked to the door leading to the basement.

Just as she was about to open the door, she heard footsteps. She turned quickly. It was Tibo.

"You're such a mule head," Aurora said in the tiniest of whispers. "What are you doing here?"

"I want to play your game," said Tibo.

"It's not a game, and how did you get by the Noise Policeman?"

"I told him I had to piddle."

"Well, then, you can go tell him you're finished and get back inside."

"No I want to stay with you. I don't like sitting by myself."

Aurora was getting desperate. They couldn't stand here forever arguing. She was getting cold and time was running out.

"If you make me go back, I'll tell Mother," Tibo threatened. Aurora wanted to push him into the snow bank. She stuffed her hands into her pockets instead. "All right. But only if you do exactly as I say."

"What's that?" asked Tibo.

"Help me find the treasure. Come, Tibo." Slowly, Aurora opened the basement door.

Tibo looked down the stairs. He was afraid of the dark.

"It's all right," said Aurora. I'll hold your hand."

They each put one cautious foot on the first stair, Tibo clinging to Aurora with one hand and feeling the wall with the other. The stairs led to a hallway, and at the end of the hallway was a beam of light. And a sound. The sound of singing.

"She's here!" whispered Aurora.

Aurora raced down the hallway toward the light, pulling Tibo along, until they reached the open door. She peeked inside. She couldn't believe her eyes. Sergeant Goth and Constable Callo of the Noise Police were standing by the Song Spinner. They were listening to the music.

"A noise machine," said Callo "What will they think of next?"

Callo picked up the magic key and examined it. An odd look came over him. Because he was holding the key, Aurora knew he was about to speak the truth. "What a thing of beauty," he said. "It should be spared."

"What?" said Goth, his eyes wide with surprise.

Then Callo began to sing along with the Song Spinner. Well, it wasn't really singing because his voice was low and rough and out of tune. Sergeant Goth looked in horror as Callo waved his arms back and forth.

"Have you lost your wits, man?" said Goth.

But Callo continued to sing. He even shuffled his feet across the floor in an awkward dance of his own invention. Thinking his comrade had gone berserk, Goth gave him a good sharp smack across the back.

The key flew from Callo's hand, and when Goth picked it up, he, too, began to sing along with the Song Spinner in a high, tenor voice. Then Callo put his arm around Goth's shoulder, and they warbled a duet.

"I didn't know noise could be so much fun."

"Yes," agreed Goth. "This wonderful machine should not be delivered up to that madman."

"But he's waiting for us to bring it to him. So it can burn with the others."

Goth winked and handed Callo an empty crate. "Captain Nizzle is in such a state, he'll never know the difference."

Aurora grabbed Tibo and led him back up the dark hallway. He had been playing with Grundle, and as she pulled him inside a large cupboard, it fell from his hand. The cupboard was hot and stuffy and dark. Aurora put her eye up to the keyhole. She could see the shadowy figures of Goth and Callo in the flickering light. They were laughing.

Aurora noticed something else through the hole. It was Grundle rolling across the floor. Right toward Sergeant Goth. She turned to Tibo. He was about to start crying when Aurora clamped her hand over his mouth. She heard laughing again.

"One of these days," said Goth, "he's going to arrest someone for wearing a loud shirt." More laughter. Goth shut the door to the storage room, locked it and placed the key above the door frame. Grundle rolled past his boot and bumped against the door without a sound. Aurora watched them disappear with the lamp and the empty crate. Soon, the sound of their footsteps faded. All was silent and dark.

When Aurora pushed Tibo out of the cupboard, he ran to pick up Grundle. Aurora stood at the door and looked up at the ledge. She had to find a way to reach the storage room key and get back to the Song Spinner. She pulled the Hush Cloth off her mouth and opened the canvas sack. She removed the matches and lit the candle. "Hold this," she told Tibo. "Quickly. We must get back before Father notices we're gone."

In the candlelight, she saw a square shape against the corner. A wooden box, the kind that oranges come in. If she stood on that, she should be able to reach the top of the door frame. But when she stood on the box, she was still too short. Even on tiptoe, her hand didn't reach high enough.

Her arm brushed something along the wall. Metal. Long and thin. A candle snuffer. She tugged at it, and it came off the wall. Now she would be able to reach the top of the door frame. She stretched her arm as far as she could and moved the snuffer across the ledge.

"Almost. Pretty close ... whoops, too far," said Tibo, holding the candle and running back and forth below her.

Aurora tried again, more slowly this time, so the snuffer wouldn't skip over the key. Near the center of the ledge, she heard a tiny ping. The snuffer had caught the key. She gave it a slight push, and the key fell off the door frame.

"Goodie ghostie," said Tibo. But Aurora knew something had gone wrong. When the key should have hit the floor with a plunk, there was only silence. She looked down and saw what she had not seen before. In the floor was a black metal grate with holes—just the right size for a key to fall through.

"Feathers!" whispered Aurora. She leaped off the box and tried to poke the snuffer into the metal grate. It was too big to go through the narrow space.

She dropped the snuffer, put her fingers into the grate and tried to lift it, but she couldn't get a proper grip.

Above her head the floorboards creaked under the Sunwatch dancers. The dance would soon be over. She sat down on the wooden box, crossed her arms and sighed.

Tibo sat next to her on the box. He was rolling Grundle along the floor. Aurora watched out of the corner of her eye. Maybe that old thing would come in handy after all.

She took the knife from her sack, reached for the string ball and cut a long piece of twine. Tibo quickly rescued Grundle and held on tight in case Aurora had any more plans for it. Then Aurora doubled the twine, doubled it again and knotted each end. She tugged hard. She had a good, strong rope.

She dropped the rope down through the grate, stuck two fingers in and pulled the rope up the other side of the metal slot. She stood over the grate and tugged. The grate held fast.

She tried again. Harder this time, until she heard a scraping sound. The grate had lifted. She stuck her hand into the shaft and poked around among the dust balls and grit.

"Hold the candle over here," whispered Aurora. Tibo held the candle above the grate.

Now she felt it. Hard, cold metal. The storage room key. She slid the grate back in place and put the key into the lock of the storage room door. She opened the door, rushed to the Song Spinner and ran her hand over the bird with the turquoise feathers.

Tibo skipped around her. "We found the hidden treasure. We found the hidden treasure."

"Now we must hide it," said Aurora. The doll carriage was just the right size.

Suddenly, the sound of dancing feet stopped. The Sunwatch dance was over. "We must get back before Father notices," said Aurora. She ran to the door to see if the hallway was clear. No! A shaft of light illuminated the stairs. Someone was coming into the basement.

Aurora shut the door and looked around the room for an escape. There were two other doors. She tried the first one. It was locked. She put the key into it. The door opened into a closet stuffed with so many boxes there was room enough for only one of them. She pushed Tibo inside, put her finger to her lips and shut the door. She unlocked the other door and looked around the dimly lit room. A table, a bed, a window with bars. She would hide the Song Spinner in here. Then a shadow moved across the floor. And a hand came from behind and covered her mouth.

CHAPTER FOURTEEN

urora's heart skipped a beat. She felt almost as if she had stopped breathing. How could she have gotten herself into this mess?

She could be upstairs right now listening to her father. He would be speaking the opening words of the Sunwatch. "Welcome all you who gather for this most solemn occasion," he would be whispering. "To-night, we celebrate the rebirth of our glorious sun."

But no, she was here, in a basement room with bars on the window and someone's hand over her mouth. She heard the door close.

She tried to wriggle away when she heard a voice whisper in her ear. A voice she had heard for the first time only two days ago but which she had come to love.

"It's all right," she heard Zantalalia say. Aurora turned and threw her arms around the old woman, but before she could tell her all the things she had discovered, she heard the faint sound of the Sunwatch Hymn playing on the Song Spinner in the next room.

Zantalalia opened the door slightly to have a look. There, listening to the music, tears streaming down his face, was Frilo the Magnificent. "But I thought he hated music," whispered Aurora, peeking through the crack in the door.

"Frilo is the one who gave me the Song Spinner," said Zantalalia. "And now 1 will have a chance to speak with him."

"No," whispered Aurora. "He was spying on us. He was the one who had you arrested. I don't want him to see me."

She looked around the room for a hiding place. She was safely under the bed when Frilo the Magnificent entered the room.

"Good evening, Lalia," he said.

"Good evening, Frilo," said Zantalalia. And Aurora wondered how she must feel, after all these years, meeting the man she had once loved. He must have been different then, decided Aurora. Handsome maybe. And nice. Zantalalia couldn't have liked him if he hadn't been nice. From under the bed, she could see Frilo. His eyes were glistening. He held something in his hand. A letter. She recognized the pink wax on the envelope. It was the letter she had written. "Did you have anything to do with this?" he asked.

"I believe I did, Frilo. Does it mention music at the Sunwatch?"

"Yes. But, of course, that's impossible," Frilo said. "It's against the Hush Law."

"You created the Hush Law. You can change it."

"Oh, dear. Oh, my. That's true. I must sit down," said Frilo. He headed for the bed and sat down, his weight pressing the sagging springs onto Aurora's head.

"It was the only way to get some peace and quiet around here," said Frilo. "Things were so noisy in the old days."

"But there was joy, Frilo. So much joy."

"I did what was best. I created a better world," said Frilo.

"You destroyed the beautiful world that was already here."

Frilo shifted his weight, and the springs moved over Aurora's head. "I did it for my people," he said.

Zantalalia stamped her foot on the stone floor. "You betrayed your people," she said. "You let this monster of a Nizzle take charge, while you passed the day taking care of ... your stomach. This is not the Frilo I once knew."

"Oooh," moaned Frilo, clutching his head with both hands.

"A headache?" said Zantalalia, her voice softening. "I remember the cure." And she gestured to a chair in the middle of the room. Frilo got up from the bed slowly. Aurora's eyes closed in relief as the bed springs lifted off her head.

When she opened them again, she saw Frilo sitting in the chair, sighing. Zantalalia was massaging his forehead and singing a soothing melody. Then she stopped singing, and in a grave voice, she asked, "What do you plan to do about this darkness, Frilo?"

"I don't know," said Frilo. "Oh, gracious. It's so troublesome. Perhaps it's even too late. Oh! I'm much too old for this. I have nothing more to say about the matter."

"Why don't you let the Song Spinner say it for you?"

"The Song Spinner?"

"Yes. Take the Song Spinner up to the Whispering Hall. And play it so that everyone—not just you—but everyone can hear the Sunwatch Hymn."

Frilo opened his eyes wide. "What a preposterous idea," he said. Zantalalia placed her fingers gently over his eyes to close them. She began to hum again.

Aurora listened from under the bed. That was the answer.

She would take the Song Spinner upstairs! She crawled out from under the bed and made a wide arc to the door, so she wouldn't be noticed. She shut the door quietly behind her. Then she walked over to the closet door and opened it. Tibo fell out, gasping for air. "I don't want to play this game anymore," he moaned.

"But we have the treasure, Tibo," she said, helping him to his feet. "Now we must show it to the others."

They took hold of the Song Spinner and carried it very slowly, very carefully up the stairs. Outside, a thick carpet of new snow awaited them. To distract the Noise Policeman at the front door, Tibo made a large snowball and threw it as far as he could. It struck a lamp, and the Noise Policeman went around the corner to investigate.

"Now, Tibo," Aurora whispered.

They picked up the Song Spinner again and rushed to the front door. Suddenly, Constable Callo appeared from the other side. "Hold on," he said. "You can't bring that in here."

Aurora heard the sound of breaking glass. She saw Zantalalia waving at her through the broken window of the basement cell. Then she heard Zantalalia begin to sing. The mosquito song. A song full of the whining sounds of a thousand hungry mosquitoes.

Aurora saw Frilo at the window, too. He was slapping at invisible mosquitoes. "Help, help," he yelled out the window. "Someone help (*slap*) get me out of (*slap*) here." (*slap, slap*) "Stop! (*slap*) I give up."

And Callo, who was just about to grab the Song Spinner, doubled over and began slapping furiously at his arms, his face, his back, his legs. Before Tibo could also come under the spell of Zantalalia's song, Aurora told him to stuff the Hush Cloth into his ears. So while Callo was busy with the imaginary mosquitoes, Aurora slipped into the Whispering Hall with the forbidden music machine. Tibo held the door open and followed behind her.

Captain Nizzle was on the stage. He was finishing his Sunwatch address. "Peaceful citizens of Pindrop," he said, "do not fear. Do not cower in the darkness. With this cleansing fire, I will achieve mastery over the evil forces that have plagued us. I will challenge the darkness to battle. I will be victorious."

Then he clenched his teeth and hissed. "There will be quiet. There will be order. There will be perfect peace in Pindrop."

Aurora and Tibo waited nervously at the entrance. By now the Song Spinner weighed a ton.

Then Captain Nizzle's voice became sweet—sweet as maple syrup. "My most sincere wish for you in the new year is this," he said. "May all your nights be silent nights."

Everyone stood up. Aurora and Tibo walked behind the backs of the crowd, so they couldn't be seen. With a sense of relief, they placed the Song Spinner on a small table laden with Sunwatch presents. Aurora inserted the magic key and let Tibo turn it three times to the left. She pulled a golden knob, and soon the wonderful bird was flying again.

And for the first time in many years, the Whispering Hall was alive with the music of the Sunwatch Hymn.

Everyone turned to listen. Aurora could see their faces now. The older ones had tears in their eyes. Was it joy or sadness, she wondered. The children's faces shone with excitement and perhaps fear. There were also a few angry faces. Captain Nizzle's was one of them.

He leaped from the stage and marched down the aisle toward them. "Who dares to disturb the Sunwatch in such a flagrant manner?" He was shouting now. He ordered everyone to sit down, and when they did, Aurora saw her father on the stage, his eyes dark with worry. She noticed the other adults shifting in their chairs. Some looked questioningly at each other. No one had ever heard the Captain of the Noise Police raise his voice before.

She could feel Tibo trembling next to her. She took his hand and realized hers was shaking, too.

At this moment, Sergeant Goth and Constable Callo entered the Hall. Callo was still scratching imaginary mosquito bites. Captain Nizzle glared and walked past them to the music machine. He brought his hand down so hard on top of the Song Spinner that the bird came to a sudden halt, and the music stopped. The silence that followed was the most terrible thing Aurora had ever heard.

She squeezed Tibo's hand tightly and took a deep breath.

Then she heard singing again. Only this time she realized it was coming from her. She was singing the Sunwatch Hymn.

"Quiet!" screamed Captain Nizzle. Aurora and Tibo were both startled at the sound. "I'll have you sent to the Water World," he howled. "But, first I will teach you a lesson you will never forget." He waved his fist in the air and was about to strike Aurora when her mother stepped between them.

"Out of my way," said Captain Nizzle.

"What was done to my father you will never do to my daughter," said Megla the Dressmaker as she stood by her children.

"And who will stop me?" asked Captain Nizzle.

"I will," said Selmo the Whisperer from the stage. But he wasn't whispering.

Captain Nizzle began to laugh. "You and your wife will stand against the great powers of the Noise Police? Ha, ha, ha, ha, ha!"

His laughter stopped short when a strong voice echoed through the Whispering Hall. "You may have great powers, Captain Nizzle," the voice said. "But we are the light. You will not put us out."

On the stage stood Zantalalia wearing the golden shawl, the one she had worn in the Circle of Stones, the one that had belonged to the grandmothers. It sparkled as if it were on fire. The birdcage was at her feet. And although it appeared to be empty to everyone else, Aurora thought she could see Doremi inside the cage.

"Who allowed that criminal into this holy place?" Captain Nizzle screamed. Aurora watched as hands flew up to protect ears unaccustomed to such outbursts.

Frilo the Magnificent, who had been standing behind Zantalalia, moved forward. "I asked Zantalalia to join me here tonight," he said. "This is where she belongs." There was a great gasp from everyone in the Hall. They could hardly believe their ears.

"She has cast a spell over you, Excellency," said Captain Nizzle. And he pointed to Goth. "Seize her at once and return her to the cell."

"Enough," said Frilo. "Please, everyone, sit down. I wish to speak to all of you." He stood quietly for a moment before he began to speak. "A long time ago, I was in love with a woman. A woman with a beautiful voice. I asked her to marry me, to sing her wonderful songs only for me. She refused. She told me her voice was a gift she would share with everyone."

Frilo looked at Zantalalia. Aurora could see the pain in his eyes. "Every note she sang became another nail in my heart," he said. "I couldn't bear the idea that others would listen to her beautiful voice, a voice that should have been all mine. And so I made up the Hush Law. I never wanted to hear the sound of her music, of anyone's music again. Now I see that my jealousy has plunged our land into darkness." Frilo pointed to Aurora at the back of the hall. "I am grateful to this child for giving me a chance to redeem myself. I ask all of you for your forgiveness. I hope I am not too late."

Zantalalia joined him at the front of the stage. "I beg you to sing tonight," she said, "with all your hearts. Sing so that we might bring the light back to our land."

"NEVER!" cried Captain Nizzle in a rage. "I would rather see this whole place burn to the ground." He snatched an oil lamp from the wall and waved it menacingly. "Men! Prepare for battle. Remove the torches. Set fire to the noise makers. Arrest anyone who tries to interfere with the Law."

The Noise Policemen looked at each other. No one moved. "Sergeant Goth!" said Captain Nizzle. "Rally the men." But Sergeant Goth stood still.

"You are no longer in charge here, Nizzle," said Frilo. "Sergeant Goth, arrest this man and take him to the Quiet House. He will be the very last tenant of that awful place. And release Lorio and Larch and all the others, so they may return to their families."

Goth and Callo took Nizzle by the arms and dragged him from the Whispering Hall. "You haven't heard the last of me," he yelled as he looked back. Perhaps not, thought Aurora. But she could see that many in the Whispering Hall that night were shocked at how much they had heard from the enforcer of the Hush Law.

The great door closed, and there was peace once again. Frilo asked everyone to remove their Hush Cloths. Some were afraid, at first, but soon they all showed their faces. There were even a few smiles. Frilo gave the sign to Aurora's father to continue the ceremony. He spoke the words that had been used to celebrate the Sunwatch for thousands of years. He tried not to whisper, but he choked on the sound. He looked to Zantalalia. She smiled, and together they chanted, "Tonight we greet the moon in her darkness. This darkness, which has now reached the limit of its power over our land."

Zantalalia took a candle from the wall, lit it and gave it to Frilo. She invited Aurora to come onto the stage and gave her a burning candle.

Selmo continued, and his voice rang like a bell. "We celebrate the rebirth of our glorious sun as it emerges from the womb of the night."

Zantalalia began to sing the Sunwatch Hymn. Aurora quickly joined in. At the end of the song, others took candles from the walls and passed them to their neighbors. When they had all received a candle, they walked out into the winter night to watch for the sun, Aurora at the head of the procession with Zantalalia. They moved slowly and gracefully, their candles flickering against the gray snow.

Zantalalia stopped for a moment, sang the first few words of the Sunrise Song and continued walking. Aurora had learned the song from the Song Spinner, so she added her voice, as did Frilo, who had never forgotten it, and a few older ones who remembered the music from their youth.

Some who had been musicians in the old days of Shandrilan broke from the procession and took up their instruments from the jumbled pile in the Great Square. They began to play. They fiddled and tooted and drummed. But the sound they made was nothing like the music of the Song Spinner.

Aurora wanted to put her fingers in her ears. Yet she was grateful that there were still a few who remembered how to play the music makers, and she felt sure they would improve with practice. One old man picked up Grandfather Jessup's horn and began to blow into it. Aurora touched the locket at her throat and smiled.

But where was the sun? There was still no sign of it.

The people released from the Quiet House came over the hill—Lorio, Larch and the others. Everyone was singing now. Even the children had learned the song. There had not been this much sound in Pindrop for many, many years.

Yet, still there was no light.

Zantalalia removed her golden shawl and put it around Aurora's shoulders. It was made of fine, delicate cloth and seemed to radiate heat, as if the love of all the grandmothers had been woven into each golden thread.

"Sing, my darling," said Zantalalia.

And Aurora did. She sang as if her life depended on it. She made up for all those years of whispering, years when she had pretended not to hear the sounds, when she had forced herself to be silent.

She felt every muscle in her body relax for the first time.

She knew that the song she was singing was coming from a place deep inside her, rising until it swelled in her throat and flew out into the darkness.

And as she sang, she thought she saw the snow changing color. No longer a dull gray, it seemed to be, yes, it was, pink. Aurora turned to look at the others. Zantalalia had pink hair. Frilo had a pink beard. Her mother's blue coat had turned purple, and everyone had scarlet faces.

The whole world was changing.

Then the sky turned from pink to blue, and there at the horizon was a golden sliver. The sun was rising above the hill. Aurora could feel her hopes rising with it, hopes for the future of Shandrilan.

She stopped for a moment and listened to the music, this most wonderful music, as it welcomed a new day. And she heard the sound she had first heard on the morning of her birthday. The beautiful sound of Zantalalia's voice. Singing.

ISBN 1425174b2-0

9 781425 174620